Things
TO DO WHEN
It's
RAINING

Also by Marissa Stapley:

Mating for Life

MARISSA STAPLEY

Things
TO DO WHEN
It's
RAINING

GRAYDON
HOUSE

GRAYDON
HOUSE

Recycling programs
for this product may
not exist in your area.

ISBN-13: 978-1-525-89901-0

Things to Do When It's Raining

GraydonHouseBooks.com
BookClubbish.com

Printed in U.S.A.

For my grandparents:

Margaret Jean and Ron Soper
Lawrence Greenman
Margaret (McKay-McLeod) and Raymond Stapley

"In rivers, the water that you touch is the last
of what has passed and the first of that
which comes; so with present time."

—Leonardo da Vinci

"I, too, seem to be a connoisseur of rain, but it does not fill me with joy;
it allows me to steep myself in a solitude I nurse like a vice I've refused to vanquish."

—Julia Glass, *Three Junes*

*V*irginia has always loved the rain. She never hides inside: she goes fishing or for a walk, and she doesn't mind getting wet. Even now, when she knows that rain means danger, she tilts her face up to meet the droplets. The fear retreats for a moment. But then she lowers her head and keeps on across the ice, faster now because she knows she must find her husband, somewhere out on this river, and save him before it's too late.

In the distance, she hears what sounds like a gunshot: the ice surrendering. If she'd known it was going to rain, she'd have gone for help. Usually, she feels it coming. But this time the clouds gathered and she didn't notice. There were bigger things on her mind. And now that she's out on the river she can't turn back. He needs her. The river, which tells her where the biggest fish are when she goes out in her boat, which tells her so many other things because she listens, is telling her now that Chase is in danger.

She's known everything about Chase since the moment he stepped off his family's yacht and onto her family's dock six years ago. She tossed her braid over her shoulder, rolled her eyes and helped him tie a proper sailor's knot, and then he looked straight into her and said, "Thank you," but he meant other things and the world stopped spinning for a minute. Later he told her he felt an axis tilt, a realignment of planets. He saw a constellation of freckles on her nose. She fell in *love with him because he said stuff like that to her. None of the boys in Alexandria Bay talked that way.*

And now he needs her. She knows.

It would be the same if their daughter were in danger: the river would whisper the threat in her ear and she would go find Mae. But their girl is out of harm's way, up in the attic of Virginia's parents' inn, also her home, playing with her friend Gabriel, oblivious to the ice that is shifting and about to crack in her world.

There's another splitting sound in the distance just as Virginia approaches Island 51. She stops and looks at the shack with its boarded-up windows. She's afraid to move, afraid to stay still. Pointless to even try, but maybe Jonah Broadbent is her only hope. Part of her still believes in this boy she once knew—now a broken man—so she climbs the slippery bank, scrambles up the stairs and pounds on the door of the shack, but then doesn't bother to wait for an answer. It's unlocked, as always, so she turns the knob and walks in.

PART ONE

Things TO DO WHEN *It's* RAINING
A list by Virginia Summers,
Junior Proprietor (self-proclaimed)
of Summers' Inn, Alexandria Bay, New York

Is there someone at home you miss?

Write her a letter and say it.

Don't wait; tomorrow it might not be raining.

On the morning Mae woke and Peter was missing, she had been dreaming she was chasing her childhood friend Gabe through the farmer's field with the steep slope where they used to go tobogganing. It was night and the moon was full, and the river was in the distance, invisible but ever present, and every time she almost reached him, she stumbled on a root, she fell, and he just kept running ahead. He would never have done that when they were kids, though; he would have turned back and reached for her hand, pulled her up—wouldn't he have? "Why do I still believe you're good?" she had shouted at his retreating form before waking and reaching for Peter.

But she was on the couch, not in their bed.

She sat up, listened, found only the silence that cloaks a space when the person being waited for hasn't come home. (Sometimes, people go out and don't come back. Sometimes, bad things happen. Mae has known this since she was six.)

Peter. Her partner. Where was he? She searched the apartment, but there was no sign of him. All thoughts and memories of Gabe vanished, all warmth from sleep was replaced with fear. She pictured a black gypsy cab running Peter down. A mugging, maybe even a heart attack. She tried his phone:

no answer. She walked through the apartment again, slowly, and found herself cataloging the items that were hers. It was somehow calming, this evidence of her presence in his home, in his life: the painting of the Saint Lawrence River on one wall; a vase near the door in a fox-hunt pattern that she used as an umbrella stand, just like the one her grandmother kept at the door of the inn where Mae was raised; the artist's rendering of Summers' Inn itself, hanging in the hallway; and the photocopied list, tucked into her dresser drawer, a replica of the one that still hung on a corkboard in the lobby of the inn, an artifact from when Mae's mother, Virginia, was alive. *What would my mother say to me if she were here now? She would tell me to get out of here and go figure out where Peter is.*

Mae went to the office in a taxi. *Maybe he's fallen asleep at his desk.* The thought reassured her, calmed her heart.

But when she arrived, she found his office empty, the entire floor devoid of life—or so she thought.

First, she found the note, tucked into her Columbia Business School coffee cup:

> Mae: I'm sorry. And I want you to know you meant something to me. You won't be implicated; WindSpan had nothing to do with you. And I won't forget you.
> L,
> Peter
>
> P.S. Please destroy this.

The world went black at first. The note was evidence that he wasn't hurt or dead. But this, in a perplexing way, was worse. Mae studied the sentences scrawled on company letterhead like an anthropologist interpreting markings on a cave wall. This was the man she had planned to marry. This was the life she had wanted to lead. And yet she had not allowed herself to see it coming.

And now, here she is. At the beginning of the end.

Mae opens her computer and logs in to the main server. How many lives has he destroyed? How many has *she* destroyed, by proxy? Will there be anything she can do to make it right? *Please let there be something I can do to make it right.*

Her fingers fly. She opens files; she reads. It's all there, and it's absurd, how easy it is to piece together. As if he wanted her to figure it out. Or—and this is a thought that spins the room, roils her stomach, brings bile to her throat—as if he didn't bother to hide it from her because he knew she'd be too stupid, too trusting, to ever check.

WindSpan Turbine does not exist. It never existed. But the money did. And now it's gone.

She abandons her computer and goes into his office again. She sits at his desk watching the sun rise over Brooklyn Bridge Park. Less than twelve hours earlier she was buying take-out ramen, carrying it home along with a six-pack of Peter's favorite microbrew. She'd remembered the hot sauce, she'd experienced and felt guilty about the smug joy that can accompany being needed by another person while passing people on the sidewalk who are possibly not needed by anyone at all. She'd set the coffee table, she'd put the ramen in glass bowls in the oven to keep it warm while she waited for him to get home from the office. She'd called him. "Something unexpected came up. I'll be home as soon as I can," he told her. Eventually, she'd fallen asleep watching Netflix.

Now she looks away from the park and down at the yellow diamond on her left ring finger. It belonged to his mother, Peter had told her, in a voice hoarse with heartbroken reverence. When Peter spoke of his family she felt like she was listening to a Southern gothic novel: tragedy and romance, privilege gone sour, a murky history involving a plantation, slaves, family secrets. Sex, lies and a damaged boy. She would heal him with her love, she had decided at some point, perhaps the minute she met him. This time, with this man, she would succeed.

She takes off the ring and puts it on top of the note. They'd gone to see a brownstone on the weekend. There's an expensive white dress hanging in her closet. Her biggest concern lately had been finding the perfect shoes. Who had she become?

She hears a whimper and can't believe she doesn't recognize the sound of her own crying. But then she realizes it's Bud. "You asshole, you left your dog behind!" The dog—named after Bud Fox from the movie *Wall Street*—is lying in the corner on a canine bed covered in toile-patterned fabric. Mae picked it because it reminded her of the curtains in her childhood bedroom at the inn. She stands; Bud woofs and scrambles toward her.

"Okay, Bud. Come on."

She once found the name of the dog endearing but now she adds it to the list of things that should have alerted her to the fact that Peter is a criminal: Bud Fox, pure intentions or not, ended up in jail. "Come on, we'll go for a walk." Bud wags his tail and romps around her, knocking her back into the chair. He's not a city dog; he's a dog who should have many acres upon which to roam. But he's the same kind of dog Peter had on the ruined plantation as a child.

Peter said the dog from his childhood—named Earl—was the one positive memory he had extracted from his youth. Until the dog had been hit by a train while out walking with Peter's suicidal twin brother not too long ago. "You were so

lucky," he had told Mae, "to have had such an idyllic upbring-
ing at that inn, with grandparents who loved you so much."

"But…my parents died when I was six." In that moment,
she thought maybe he'd forgotten, but he'd waved a hand,
nodded. No, he hadn't forgotten.

"You were so young you can't remember them. How can
you pine for something you never really had?"

These words had hurt her, deeply and swiftly. What she
had wanted to say was "I remember everything—and yet, I
remember nothing. You can't imagine how much that hurts.
Sometimes, I wake from a dream and I know it was a memory,
but it slips away from me like a fish down an ice hole. And
no matter how hard I try, I can't get it back. Except there is
one memory that, no matter what, I can't shake: the last time
I saw my father. What I said, what I did, what I caused. I've
never told anyone, but—" Even when she's only imagining
her confession, though, she can't finish the sentence. So she
buries it, back in the place where it lives, deep down in the
riverbed of her soul. She had actually believed that Peter was
good for her, because he didn't allow her to wallow, to dwell
in the past.

Bud is nuzzling her hand; she clips the leash onto his collar. He resembles an old man: gray, bedraggled, hair growing
out of his ears. She suddenly imagines Peter leaving a note
for Bud, maybe tucked under his dog bed. *You meant something to me, Bud. And I'm sorry. Please eat this note.* She shoves
her own note, and her engagement ring, into the pocket of
her jeans and thinks about what she's going to do with the
scrap of paper. Burn it, maybe. And the ring? She'd throw
it into the Hudson except she's probably going to need the
money she'll get from selling it to pay for a lawyer. The note
said she wouldn't be implicated, but there's no reason to trust
Peter's words.

As she walks through the office again, she considers running. Just running away. But that would be an admission of guilt—and she did not do this. Besides, she knows she could never live with herself if she ran, if she hid, from a crime that was not hers but a crime she presided over no less. She pauses and looks into the office of Andrew, the CFO, but it's as silent and empty as Peter's. Something is missing: he kept a paperweight made of meteor rock on his desk, but now there's a dust-free circle where it used to sit. "It reminds me that the world could end at any second, so I might as well live it up," he said to her once, trying to explain why he was dating a twenty-five-year-old waitress he met at Hooters. She has the urge to sweep her arm across his desk and crash everything left on it to the ground.

The elevator opens as she pushes the down button, and Bridget, one of the account managers, steps off. "Morning!" she says.

"Oh, hi!" It comes out as a shout.

"Hey, is Peter here?"

"Not yet."

"Can we chat? I got a strange call from Alex Moffatt last night. I tried to get in touch with Peter, but his phone is off and—"

"Definitely!" Mae tugs Bud onto the elevator, hard. This is not an easy dog to bend to your will. "I'll be right back." She hits the button for the door to close and keeps pressing it until finally the doors shut. Outside with Bud, she rolls the sleeves of her sweater down over her hands and squints against the winter sunlight. Bud leads her to the park. Once he's inside the fence, she unclips his leash and he runs off, first lifting his leg against a fence post and then walking a few paces away to squat, lowering his head modestly. She sinks down onto a bench and feels the cold dampness seep through the seat of her jeans.

"Mae?" She looks up. It's Jon Evans, a lawyer who works nearby and lives with his wife, Mattie, in Williamsburg, the same neighborhood where Mae and Peter live. They have a baby named Jorja. Mae held her once, at the office. She remembers Jon explaining that Mattie had become ill shortly after Jorja was born. Non-Hodgkin's lymphoma; she had a kerchief over her head when she visited the office. She still looked beautiful, vibrant, even with her pale skin and high cheekbones in sharp relief against her face, but there had been something in her eyes that had made Mae want to reach out and squeeze her hand. Peter had been overbright to make up for it.

"This is my wife," he had said to Jon. "Or—soon to be. She takes care of the marketing for us." How Mae had loved those two words: *my wife*. In them, she had seen a future that did not involve her dying alone because she had no family— a viable concern when your only two living relatives (that you've ever met, at least) are in their eighties. "Do you want kids?" she had asked Peter when they had been dating long enough for her to bring it up. She had feared the answer: so many men didn't, or said they didn't until it was too late and then had babies with women who had not been left on the shelf so long that they were reproductively challenged. "Of course I want kids," he had said. "That's a silly question."

She had envisioned inviting Jon and Mattie to dinner parties, had looked into Jorja's eyes and prayed then that Mattie would be all right, that Jorja would not have to spend her life picking over her memories of her mother until they were almost gone. She had imagined Jorja playing with these future babies, the ones that would save her; she had imagined a perfect world.

Jon and Mattie had invested a huge amount of money in WindSpan Turbine. And now she can't look Jon in the eye. "Mae? Are you all right?" She realizes the silence has stretched too thin, that she's staring blankly over his left shoulder. She forces herself to meet his gaze head-on.

"How's Mattie?"

"Strong. Hopeful. Better every day. She's an amazing woman."

Mae imagines hospital bills that can't be paid. She calls for Bud. "I'm sorry," she says to Jon. "I'm not feeling well. Really, *really* not feeling well."

"Can I do anything?"

"No. But thanks. I need to get back to the office now. Or maybe head home and lie down."

"That's probably a good idea; you look pale. Hey, but sorry—can you have Peter call me when he gets a sec? I need to double-check something with him. I saw something on Twitter last night that was a bit concerning. About WindSpan. An article that seemed to suggest the site was abandoned. Or…not even abandoned, not even *there*. I'm sure that can't be. Probably just trolls, or whatever, but I wanted to check in, so I'm glad I ran into you."

Mae's hand trembles as she attaches the leash to Bud's collar. "Of course, will do, try not to worry, I'm sure it's nothing." As she walks away, she realizes she's forgotten something. Let that be added to the catalog of her transgressions: *And she walked away without even picking up her dog's shit.*

Back at the office, a knot of people have gathered. They are silent as she approaches. "I'm surprised you came back," says Josh, who answers the phones. "I thought you'd taken off, too." Josh is looking at her with revulsion and pity and something else. Because she was Peter's fiancée, which means she either knew about this—in which case she's a horrible person—or did not—in which case she's a fool. *I'm both*, she wants to say. *And I'm so sad, and I'm so sorry.*

The elevator doors open behind her. A man and a woman emerge. They are plain clothed, but as their hands go into their jacket pockets, Mae knows they're reaching for police badges. She reaches into her own pocket and feels for the note. She crumples it tighter, tries to make it small enough not to exist, but the ring gets in the way.

Eat! Go to Coffee Pot Cathy's for the best fish sandwich you've ever had, Lil' River Fudge Co. for... well, obviously fudge, and the Bay Area Bakery for amazing bagels. (And start planning your fishing camp shore lunch for when it stops raining. I can help!)

Gabe is at a restaurant he's never been to and knows he'll never go to again. He'll probably avoid this block entirely. He's with his wife, moments away from her being his ex-wife, and she's telling him he never loved her.

"You were very *fond* of me, Gabe. You *cared* about me. But loved me? No. You never loved me. You were too damaged to love me. I think you did love someone once—that girl you told me about, back when you used to talk about your childhood, what was her name, Molly?"

"Mae." Gabe mumbles it. It's too pathetic, too sad, that Natasha is right even about this.

"Yeah. Her. The only person you ever loved is a ghost, someone you'll probably never see again. And until you either make her real or exorcise her, you won't be..." She pauses and looks past him, searching for the right word. The waiter misinterprets it, thinks she's ready to order and approaches the table, but she dismisses him with a firm head shake. "Until then, you won't be whole. But that's only part of it." Now the head shaking is sad, and she falls silent, as if she can't bring herself to get into all the other ways in which he is broken. Instead, she reaches her hand across the table. "You need to know something. I'm pregnant. Twins. In vitro."

He puts both his hands under the table. "Too much information. And, it's pretty obvious. You're huge."

She sighs. "You're a dick."

"You fucked around with one of the doctors from the hospital where you work. Sorry if I'm bitter." She'd been living
with the doctor for some time, following an affair with him
that she had once lain at Gabe's feet like a challenge. *Fight for
me*, her eyes had demanded. Gabe did not. Who could com-
pete with a renowned pediatric cardiologist? She was an anesthesiologist; they were the good team. Except he *could* have
competed. Natasha had loved him. It was a gift that he had
senselessly squandered, and now there's nothing left to say.

He stares down at the table until finally she says, "So, the
papers." She pushes the folder across the table at him along
with a navy Montblanc pen, and he imagines the renowned
pediatric cardiologist giving it to her, the perfect gift. The
last thing Gabe gave her was a can opener. He'd meant it as a
joke, but it's never funny to give your wife a can opener. What
was the punch line, anyway, of the can opener joke? He can't
remember. Who cares? He gave her a fucking can opener.

"As discussed, we'll both walk away with what we walked
in with. A clean break."

He picks up the pen. He signs. It does not feel like a clean
break at all. But it does feel like an ending, and there is some
relief in that. Endings always relieve Gabe.

"You're okay, right? Still freelancing? I saw one of your
drawings in the *Times*."

"There. Done." He signals for the bill, then remembers
they haven't ordered anything yet. He picks up his water glass,
swigs. It's not what he needs. He stands.

"Gabe, please, don't go yet. You can't run away from everything for the rest of your life. We should—"

"Goodbye, Natasha."

He doesn't run, he walks, so she's wrong about that at least. He buys Wild Turkey on the way to his new apartment and drinks some in the elevator, then collapses with the bottle onto the mattress on the floor, the mattress he dragged up three flights of stairs by himself even though friends offered to help him move. He can afford better than this shithole. When she asked he could have told her that, yes, his freelance career is doing just fine, that a publisher might even be interested in his kids' graphic novel idea, but he didn't bother. He stares at the ceiling. It's heavily water stained. It looks like it might collapse on him. *What would that be like*, he wonders, *to have a ceiling collapse on you? Would it be a quick death, or slow and suffocating?*

Quite the life you've carved out for yourself, Gabriel Broadbent.

Alex Bay isn't your typical tourist town. There are mysteries, secrets, a shadowy past involving pirates. And you can find out about all of it at the Cornwall Brothers Store & Museum, where, conveniently, you can also shop for souvenirs.

Lilly waits, listens, counts George's breaths, counts the spaces between them. He's asleep. She sits up, waits again, searches with her feet in the darkness for her slippers, slides them on, stands and finds her dressing gown where she left it, draped over the chair in front of the dressing table. She pauses with her hand on the chair. She used to sit here and apply her makeup before leaving this room every morning. When you were running an inn you always had to look presentable. You couldn't just wander around in slippers and a dressing gown, hair sticking out at all angles.

She backs away from the chair. A floorboard protests beneath her feet. She turns and steps on another one, and this one groans even louder. George stirs. She used to know where every creaking floorboard was in this house. Now she doesn't.

She didn't notice the forgetting at first. Names, mostly, and George had carried a piece of notepaper in his front shirt pocket for decades because he could never keep names straight in the high season, when the inn was full of strangers and old friends. She'd tried making her own cheat sheet, but it was only a month before the forgetting of names gave way to something more: an abyss of things forgotten, but not enough that you didn't feel them hovering just outside your grasp. She'd wake in the night and shout the name of a person or a town. George thought she was having nightmares. He'd rub her back to get her to sleep again, the way he used to after Virginia died.

When she shouted, "Everett!" that meant trouble. No back rub that night: George got up and wandered the house himself, though he didn't mention her outburst to her the next day at breakfast. "I keep forgetting his name, until I'm asleep," she wanted to say to him. But she knew where that would lead. George wanted to sell the inn and move to a condominium. A box beside the river, but not one that contained any of her memories. And she couldn't leave the inn, ever. She had promised Virginia. And before that, Everett.

Hadn't she promised them? Whom had she promised?

She feels her way along the wall. *Don't trip and fall and break your hip or you'll get moved into that damn condo anyway, or worse, an assisted-living home, where people will assist you right off the mortal coil.* The darkness is danger, but she can't risk turning on a light and waking George. He'll want to know why she's up. She'll have to say she can't sleep and needs a glass of warm milk, and then she'll have to make it and drink it and be up for the rest of the night peeing.

The stairs. The moonlight in the window at the bottom helps. She sits on the top step, then bumps down on her bottom, like a child—like Mae used to, and Virginia before her. *Bump. Bump. Bump.* She grips the banister and pulls herself back to standing. There.

She shuffles along the threadbare carpet, and now at least she remembers where the pitfalls are: here the floor has buckled slightly; there a floorboard is loose and popped up, a booby trap for old toes. Then she forgets where she's going and almost veers into the kitchen because the last words she can remember are *warm milk.* No: her desk, her box. *Condominium?*

Not that kind of box. The one Tommy made before he went to war. Tommy, your big brother. Tommy, who was a flyboy, and wrote to you about how much he missed the bay and about the importance of home, stability, staying in one place while you still had the chance. And so you did it for all of them: Tommy, Everett, Virginia and now Mae. Your grandchild, the only one you haven't lost, yet.

"Mae," she says, because this is a name she cannot forget, because once she forgets Mae, she's finished.

Lamplight; she opens her rolltop desk. And there is the box, right where she left it. There's such relief lately in finding things just where she left them—and such frustration when they aren't there, or worse, when she forgets what she's looking for entirely.

The box is cedar, still fragrant; there are clumsy flowers carved along the bottom. She opens it. Photos, letters, dried flowers that crumble at her touch. A birth certificate, a death notice. She slides these beneath a newspaper article featuring a photograph of her and George smiling through specks of confetti. There she is in her blue jacquard traveling suit. She had a white carrying case, and inside it…inside it— But what is that other word? What did they call them, all those things gathered up before a wedding day, items she had to scrimp and save for or make herself, because nothing was easy to come by when there was a war on?

The clock ticks. The word matters only because she can no longer recall it.

She had to get extra fabric to make those clothes, she had to allow for the slight widening of girth that no one was supposed to know about, not even her new husband, not yet.

Outside the window the river is frozen, silent, but it's silence she can hear.

What is the word?

Trousseau. It was called a bridal trousseau.

Buoyed by relief, she plunges her hand back into the box and comes up with a bundle of letters, held together by a decaying rubber band. She knows his handwriting: these were Everett's letters from the ship. She can see that he wrote "beautiful" and "love you madly, deeply" and "dream of your kisses, every night." Her cheeks grow warm. Her old cheeks, now the texture of crepe paper, can still blush like a girl's cheeks. It makes her smile. This is why she likes to go through this box: because everything in it makes her remember. "Hello, Everett," she says, into the silent dark. And then, "Hello, darling," because she's grateful to him in that moment for helping her recall who she is, who she was.

A rustling sound. Someone is standing in the door frame.

"Darling," she says to her husband, to George this time, but it has the wrong effect. She has hurt him, she can see it in his eyes, and the panic of what she has inflicted is causing her to forget what and where and why and… *"Oh."* She lifts up a photograph and holds it in front of her face. Who are those girls, so young, with foolish hair? Who is that handsome man that the most foolish-looking girl is hanging on to?

It's you. You and Vivian and Everett, and George took the photograph. Lilly drops the photo and claps her hands. How wonderful, to be able to remember that!

But someone is standing in the room. Someone who is angry with her. She stares at him, blinks uncomprehendingly. *There's an angry old man in the room*—George.

"I'm sorry." These words are automatic.

"What are you sorry for?" he asks in a hoarse, broken voice. "Are you sorry that you had to marry me and live with me all these years, instead of marrying the man you really wanted to marry?"

"I wanted to marry you!"

Trousseau. Bridal. Niagara Falls. The feeling of being saved, guilty gratitude and also so much love and hope and George. Clinging to him like he was a lifeboat. A bolt of silk my mother gave me. She'd been saving it for years, she said. In her eyes, knowledge and accusation. It was white silk, as pure as snow, and I should have handed it back to her, her eyes were daring me to say I couldn't wear white because I was already...

"Are you listening to me?"

"I can't forget him! I can't forget his name, don't you see? He was the father of my child!"

Wait. *No.*

Not the right words. That was a secret, or not exactly a secret, but something they didn't...that was a promise, or that was—

George is gone. She hears his heavy footfalls on the stairs and remembers again. She said the wrong thing. She said a secret.

She puts her head in her hands and stares down at the desk, at a photo of a young woman she no longer knows and a man she doesn't want to forget—not because she still loves him now but because she still needs him in order to remember herself. "I'm sorry," she whispers. But it's too late for sorry now.

We just got the game Clue! It's so fun.

Gather up some fellow guests and play a few rounds.

(I bet it was Colonel Mustard in the parlor with the

lead pipe.)

"How long have you known Peter Greaves?"

"About a year." *A year next week.*

Both detectives are taking notes.

"And you worked together, but you were romantically involved also?"

"We were engaged." She can picture the moment, six months ago, when Peter held out the ring. She had felt like every piece of her life had fit into place—or that her life was expanding to fit more pieces into it. They were in Paris, at the top of the Ferris wheel at the Tuileries. On the way down he had said, "Doesn't it feel like we're flying, baby?"

Everything with Peter felt spontaneous, even the proposal. *Let's take the ferry to Staten Island for lunch. Let's take a helicopter tour. Let's fly to Chicago just to have dinner. Let's make love, right here, right now. No one can see. Baby, let's get married.* She reaches into her pocket and touches the diamond ring. No one had ever called her "baby" before. At first, she didn't like it.

"Are you ready to continue?" the male detective asks. She's crying; she hadn't realized.

"Yes. I'm ready."

"Did you have any reason to believe that something wasn't right about WindSpan Turbine?"

"Yes. No. Not exactly. I mean…" She takes her hand out of her pocket and wipes both her sweaty palms on her jeans. *I really should get a lawyer. Why did I say no to that?* She breathes in deeply and continues. "I had a feeling, I think. But I—I was too afraid to say anything to Peter."

"Afraid why? Afraid that he might harm you in some way?"

She shakes her head. "Afraid, I guess, that he would leave." She says this in a voice that sounds too childlike in her own ears. "Afraid to make him angry or unhappy. Because it was very important to me to make…to make him happy. To try to make him better, a better person."

The two officers exchange a look.

"Did he leave anything behind, any sort of message for you?"

She can no longer feel her legs. Maybe she's having a panic attack. *Please destroy this.* "No. Nothing."

"And he didn't ask you to meet him anywhere?"

She can't speak. If she does, she'll break into a thousand pieces.

"Listen to me, right now." The female detective leans forward. The hostility in her tone surprises Mae and she glances at the male but he looks away from her. She wishes she could remember their names. "Do you know how many people are getting screwed here? How many people are losing money? What's going to happen to *them*? How can they get it back if *you* don't talk?"

Mae leans away and crosses her arms around herself protectively. "Okay. I'll talk. I *am* talking. I just… Sorry."

"So, did he ask you to meet him anywhere?" The male again, in his "good cop" voice but Mae does not uncross her arms.

"No."

"Did you ever wonder why Peter never cosigned on the loan for the business?"

"He said he had a problem with his credit rating because of a company he tried to start when he first graduated from college."

"Earlier, you said you had a feeling something was amiss, but nothing you could formalize. Was this just a sense he was keeping secrets from you? Or was there more to it?"

"He would often tell me that there were parts of the business I didn't need to worry about, that he was the one with the business sense. When he started it with Andrew, I asked to be more involved, for a more official title, but he avoided it. Maybe I should have fought him on that, maybe then I would have known everything. I received a merit-based fellowship at Columbia Business School every year. I made the dean's list every year, too. But... I'm sorry, I know maybe that doesn't matter, but somehow I didn't feel good enough, not smart enough. Not at Peter's level. He used to tell me my academic experience wasn't the 'real world.' I always found his disdain for higher education strange, given that he was a Harvard grad."

At this, at the mention of Harvard, the female detective raises an eyebrow and smirks. Mae feels something snap and go cold deep inside her, ice water rushing through her veins.

"I'm afraid that's not true."

"What isn't?"

"What exactly did Peter tell you about his past?"

"That he was from Charleston."

"What else?"

He told me his mother eventually developed a proclivity for drinking Hurricanes out of coffee mugs, thinking no one would know about the liquor—except the concoctions were so strong you could smell them when you walked into a room. He said she died of cirrhosis of the liver, that she would cough blood into monogrammed handkerchiefs. That his father died of a heart attack shortly thereafter, in the bed of

the housemaid, the one remaining staff member of the financially ru-
ined family. That there was not a penny left from the former empire
after his father ran it into the ground to will to Peter or his brother,
Clay—the one who later jumped in front of a train and dragged the
family dog along with him. But how could it be that a dog could live
that long? If Peter got the dog when he was five, how could it still be
alive then, when he was thirty-five?

"Look, can you just— He was lying to me, obviously. Can
you just tell me who he really was and spare me the embarrassment of telling you all the stupid stuff I believed?"

A long sigh. The male detective won't meet her eyes again,
but finally he's the one who speaks. "His real name is Bradley Matheson. He has a criminal record for fraud in Michi-
gan, which is where he was born and where he grew up. In
Novi. Father unknown, mother unemployed. He never went
to Harvard, that's for sure. He was on probation when he disappeared seven years ago. Ms. Summers, you don't look well.
Let's break now."

He faked an identity, he faked an accent, he faked a life, he faked
everything. And he didn't love me. She closes her eyes against
this thought. All of it was a lie. But only a fool would have
fallen for it. "No. Keep going." Eyes still closed, she pictures
the inn, the river, her grandparents, Lilly and George. At least
she has somewhere to go when this is all over, people to run
home to. At least she's always had, and will always have, the
inn. More than just a home. A place where everyone is welcome, no matter how broken they are. She opens her eyes
again. "Let's just get this over with. Please." *So I can go home,*
where it's safe.

Go to the Legion hall and flip through the Book of the Dead. This town had a lot of heroes in WWI and II. My Father fought in the war, with his best friend, Everett, whose name is in the Book of the Dead. Look him up. Everett Patrick Green. And my uncle Tommy is in there, too. This town lost a lot.

George can't sleep. He had too much rye at the Legion, down the road from the hotel he's staying at now. He used to pity the men who would stay so late and drink so much. Now he's one of them, a man who staggers past the *Book of the Dead* on his way out the door but is not fit to be counted among those heroes whose pictures and stories are inside. Not just because he didn't die, but because he's a coward. Even worse, he's a man living in a hotel room. He sits on the side of the bed and it creaks. There is a perpetual dampness at the corner of each of his eyes now. It doesn't go away.

On the floor at his feet is Lilly's cedar box, the one that holds all her private things: her letters, her memories, her photographs. Birth notices, death notices. All the things she has lost. *We have lost.* He feels a surge of indignation as he picks it up and places it on the bed beside him. He hears Lilly say it again in his mind: "He was the father of my child."

She finally admitted it after all these years. And she admitted more when she didn't think he was listening. Her "darling" Everett: the truth had come out. And when it did, George had allowed the anger he felt to sweep him away and up, up the stairs and into their bedroom, where he did the first thing he could think of: packed a suitcase. Five pairs of socks but only two pairs of underwear and no undershirts; this caused him fresh rage every day because he certainly couldn't go back to the inn and get them, and buying new would be a waste.

That night, the anger swept him, wavelike, back down the stairs and out the front door without a word to his wife of sixty-seven years. On his way past her, where she still sat at that desk with her head in her hands, he picked up her memory box and all the things that went in it, and he left her where she was. Because if he was leaving her, he was not leaving her alone with Everett, with his best friend, even if he was long since dead.

He had paused at the door for just a moment, and she had looked up at him. It was as if she didn't recognize him. He didn't recognize himself either, this angry man he'd become.

He walked into town; he left her the car. Let it not be said that he had left his wife in the lurch. All he had taken from her was this one thing, and he opens the lid of it now. There are flowers carved into the box, and they're crude but carved with love. Who made her this box? He bets it was Everett, a token of his adoration. He begins to sift, his new habit. Poring through the contents is like ripping off a scab: you do it even though you know the wound will only bleed and need to heal all over again. His age-spotted hand closes on a packet of letters and he eases the decaying rubber band away. He skims the first letter, dated April 18, 1940, his eyes alighting on the familiar refrains of a young soldier at the front, missing home. Then he sees his name, and reads the passage more slowly:

Thank you for the picture of my beautiful niece. Virginia is a pretty name. I'll meet her soon. And please, send my regards to George. I'm sure glad to hear those depth-charge injuries have healed up. That was a rough go. For all of you. I'm sorry.

And then this:

I think about you all the time, and about your loss. I'm sure you do, too—but I'm glad you have George now. You have a new life, sister. Make the best of it.

Now I want you to do something for me. Take that baby girl with you, my dear little niece I have yet to meet, and introduce her to the river. I swear to you I would trade anything at all just to come back home and stay in one place, forever and ever. You don't realize what you have until it's missing from your life, Lilly. Remember that.

Love,

your brother,

soon to be home (I hope),

Tommy

Hope is a funny thing, George thinks. Hope changes nothing, but you think it does until the moment you can't anymore. Tommy was shot down in the middle of the war, and for a while they said he was MIA. So everyone hoped he'd be found, and he *was* found—dead in a prison camp. Tommy was George's friend, not as close as Everett, but still...and then he was gone and no one talked about him because it hurt too much.

With a trembling hand, George puts Tommy's letter back and picks up another.

"Everett." He says it aloud, and it feels as if doing so summons a ghost. Was that the pressure of a hand on his shoulder? Was that the breath of his friend in his ear? No, not here. Everett's ghost would never haunt these decrepit hallways, these rooms that time and goodwill have forgotten.

August 4, 1939,
My beautiful Lilly, I lost your picture. We were hit by a wave and your likeness slipped overboard. I need you. I need your picture. Please send me another. When I close my eyes, your face is there. And your hair, and your smell, and the softness of your skin.

George stops reading. He feels it, as if the bed he is sitting on were moving. Waves like that the body doesn't forget. Never, no matter how many years you try to pretend you never sailed that particular sea. It all comes back.

George and Everett were on the mess deck on the corvette boat in a tiny compartment, thirty-three-by-twenty-two feet. Each man had a hammock, a locker for his clothing and a metal ditty box for his personal effects, kept in the rack above.

They had just finished their watch and gone down to the mess deck to try to sleep.

As usual, Everett had taken out his ditty box. It's what he always did: he took out the picture of Lilly and then lay on his hammock. "Georgie?" he called over, eyes still on the photo.

"Mmm?" George was pretending to read, but really he was wishing he could see that photo.

"Think she's going to wait for me?"

George was silent, staring down at the book and not seeing the words.

"George?" Everett repeated. George lowered the book.

"Of course she's going to wait. She loves you. And she's Lilly."

This said it all, didn't it? She was loyal, knowable and she belonged to Everett. Except—George closed his eyes for just a moment. Except there was the memory of her lips against his, so fast perhaps they were never really there, like butterfly wings in a dream.

"Thanks, mate," Everett said. "You're a good friend."

George felt like he was choking suddenly, on his own disloyalty, his own want for something that belonged to his best friend. His brother in arms. The day before, George had been sick over the side of the boat in some particularly rough waters, and a fellow crew member had muttered something about George being a milquetoast. Everett had the guy up against the wall so fast, spitting insults into his ear until he apologized to George and skulked away.

"You, too, Everett. You, too," George managed, then covered his mouth with his hand.

Everett frowned, concerned. "How's the gut now? Feeling okay?"

"Oh, yes, much better today."

Everett went back to looking at Lilly's photo and George went back to pretending to read. That kiss. He thought about it all the time. As a memory, it was becoming faded and frayed, because he had taken it out and pondered it so many times. They had gone for a walk the day before he was to leave. She was mostly silent, walking with him beside the river as they had so many other times. Until she stopped and said, "George, please be careful." And then her lips like rose petals against his own, and then her body, her heartbeat, her warmth, her scent. George had been rendered senseless by the unexpected combination of all the things that made her Lilly. And he had done nothing, had not even moved his lips or lifted his arms to place them on her back, had not pulled her in. Too soon, she was gone and his lips were moving against air, his hands were reaching out for nothing. He didn't want to go, he wanted to tell her he was scared, but he couldn't tell anyone because they were all scared.

He felt foolish. He had given it too much meaning. She had probably just been giving him a friendly peck, a pal's embrace. They had known each other forever, and he was going off to war. Life was not normal. Kisses didn't mean anything at times like those—or they did, but that meaning would have no place in the world when the war was over.

He closed his eyes again, about to imagine her face in Everett's photo, when the ship shuddered. *Torpedo!*

No, it was a wave. Not certain death, only the possibility of it. They were tossed from their hammocks, flung with bruising force to the floor. He knew he was going to be sick again, but managed to hold it in.

"Shit!" Everett was on the floor beside him. "You all right, George?" George saw Everett's hands, scrabbling around on the ground. For a moment he thought maybe he was hurt, but then he realized his friend had lost hold of Lilly's photo.

But there were other things to worry about. The ship was going over. The emergency alarm was screaming for all hands on deck. George spotted the photograph. He was on all fours, reaching for it—and Everett didn't see because George placed his hand over it so quickly.

"We have to go up," George said.

Everett stopped his frantic search. When he turned to head onto deck, George slipped the photo into his pocket. Then he followed his friend.

The ship rolled onto its right side, and it seemed there was nowhere else for it to go except all the way over, but it didn't somehow. George and Everett made their way out to the wheelhouse to help shore things up. As they worked, all George could think about was the photograph crammed in his pocket, wet, possibly wrecked, but there.

He should have given it back to Everett. But he did not. Not then. Not ever.

It's upstairs, at home, hidden in his old ditty box at the back of a closet. It's been there for seventy years. And Lilly has never known.

She's not the only one with secrets. And he has another one, too: he has a new friend. His friend is Jonah Broadbent. He's having breakfast with him tomorrow, and Lilly wouldn't like that. Which is partly why he's doing it—but it's not the only reason.

Play charades.

For weeks, Mae is asked to come into the police station to talk to the detectives—she calls them "Good Cop" and "Bad Cop" in her mind, depending on their mood and the day, until she finally finds their cards in the pocket of a pair of jeans she retrieves from the bedroom floor and drags over her legs one morning: detectives Nick Lamoglea and Anna Baker, from the NYPD.

Sometimes she sees coworkers passing through the doors of the station as she is coming in. Every time, she wishes for the courage to say something, but instead she looks away, ashamed. She brings Bud with her wherever she goes. At the police station, he's always at her feet.

There's a knot of anxiety in her stomach, and it's growing every day. She throws up sometimes, can manage only plain toast and tea, drinks Pepto-Bismol straight out of the bottle and congratulates herself because at least it's not vodka. One night, while she sits in the apartment—Peter's apartment, it doesn't matter how much of her stuff is in it, it's not hers and she knows that now—staring at the television, the landlord knocks and tells her the rent has not been paid for two months. He's been trying to call Peter but his phone isn't on.

"That's right," Mae says. "His phone isn't on because he committed a felony and fled the country."

The landlord blinks at her a few times, as if he's trying to decide if she's joking. "I'll get you the money. I'll have a check for you on Friday." This isn't true: she has no money because her account is frozen and she maxed out her credit cards on office furniture.

When he's gone, she returns to the couch and stares at the television again. She's not going to stay here. She needs to go home, as soon as Good Cop and Bad Cop tell her she's free. It will be quiet there. There's the past to contend with, there always is, but it will still be peaceful. The river will be frozen and silent, the town empty of tourists. She can keep herself busy by doing some of the repairs she noticed were in need of addressing when she and Peter were there at Christmas. She had been hoping he wouldn't notice, because she had painted such a pristine picture of it for him before they arrived. But how could he not have seen the water damage from a burst pipe, the aging roofs on the guest cabins, the worn carpets, that one kitchen cupboard hanging askew?

Mae puts her face in her hands. How is she going to tell her grandparents about this? They wanted more for her, she wanted more for herself, but it's not just that. They invested money in WindSpan, too. It had been her idea, but Peter had let her go through with it. And all those repairs are going to take money.

She stands, shuts off the lights and goes to bed. After she closes her eyes she hears Bud pad into the room and jump up to join her where she is lying, fully clothed. He weighs down the side that used to be Peter's, and when she reaches out, he licks her hand. And she wishes, for just a moment, that once upon a time Peter really did have a dog named Earl, that this one thing was true, that for what it was worth, maybe there was a time when he was just a boy with a dog.

Tomorrow, she'll ask the detectives how much more she has to endure. She'll ask if she can go home. As the sleeping pill she took earlier finally kicks in and halcyon drowsiness dulls the edges of her pain, she sees it, thank God, she had trouble picturing it today, during a short break at the police station when they finally left her alone: Summers' Inn, perched at the edge of the Saint Lawrence, where the water flows into the bay. She sees the yellow-gray stone walls, the navy blue shutters on every window, the red roof, the weather vane in the shape of a sturgeon. She sees it as it was, not as it is. She sees the guest cabins and the dock and the white-painted boathouse and the old gas pump. She sees the fir trees lined up along the bank, their needles the color of army fatigues in peacetime. She sees the wide-girthed oak tree with its whorled bark, the rope hanging from its thick branch. And she sees herself and Gabe, *Damn you, Gabe*, swinging and splashing, over and over, two children, best friends. She sees his little boat with the outboard motor. She sees his face. She sees the islands, the white chalk on the rocks, the numbers and the names: Blueberry. Rachel's. Half Moon. And Island 51.

In that space between wakefulness and asleep, between dream and reality, Gabe stands before her. Hope springs up, a crocus in dark earth. Maybe this time, in this dream, she'll get near enough to ask him why. Then she'll know who to look for as she scans faces without meaning to, day after day.

But, no. In her dream she is nearly buried alive in a pile of notes raining down from the sky. All of them say, "Mae, I'm sorry."

Paper airplanes are a lost art.

Try making one. It's harder than you think.

Gabe is drunk. He can hear Natasha talking to him but he knows she isn't there. *Until you either make her real or exorcise her, you won't be whole,* she says, over and over.

It's not that he doesn't want to find Mae, not that he hasn't thought about her every day forever, not that her name doesn't surface at moments he can never predict, felling him with the strength of it, the strength of *her*, even after all this time. He could look her up on the internet, he knows, but also, he can't. On the last night he spent in Alex Bay, Mae's grandmother, Lilly, had made it clear that he should stay away. Forever. And he respects it because he has to. If he had a daughter or granddaughter and a guy like him was sniffing around—well, he would have done the same thing, or worse.

But that doesn't mean he doesn't miss her, even now. That doesn't mean it doesn't hurt. Natasha is right, yet again. He loved Mae. Probably still does love her, for what it's worth.

He can remember her so easily, in all her incarnations: first, a little girl with messy curls asking him—*him!*—if he wants to come over and play; then a young girl with glasses and braces and freckles; then a teenage girl with tawny-brown eyes and a sunshine smile that one day, out of nowhere, makes him see the good in a world he always thought was against him.

Then a girl with skin that turns from ivory to pale bronze as the seasons change, like winter giving way to spring giving way to the gold of summer, except where her bathing suit straps go. There: the white lines on her shoulders, cultivated by sunlight and the straps he wants to gently push away, to reveal soft shoulders that sometimes peel after long, hot days. He came to know that skin, all of it. Indelible, the mark that skin left upon him.

He's staring at the water stains again. This is why Natasha left him. Because she knew that as soon as it was officially over between them he would end up on an epic bender, the highlight of which was thinking about someone he hasn't seen since he was eighteen.

What a fuckup he is. Maybe he should go for a walk or something, get out of this apartment, dump the bourbon down the sink, break the vicious cycle—but then his phone rings. He looks at the number, sees the area code, reflexively hits the decline button because it's an Alex Bay number and how can that even be possible? Can't be his father, whom he hasn't spoken to since he left. And it can't be...anyone else. He drinks more bourbon, gets up and starts to pace. But eventually he can't stop himself from listening to the message.

A throat clear. "Hello, Gabriel, it's George Summers calling..."

Would Gabe have recognized his voice after all these years if he hadn't said his name right away? He sounds much older, his voice a little reedy, but, yes, he would have known his voice anywhere, the cadence of his words: careful, measured, kind. "I found your number because—well." Another throat clear. Then he starts talking faster, as if he were nervous. "Your father has been carrying your number around and I thought I ought to try to get in touch because— Now he's asleep and I'm with him and... I think you need to know that

Jonah is not well. And he needs help, and I don't mean because he's been drinking. He's not drinking. I thought you'd want to know that. Gabe—the other thing is, seeing your number made me realize that... I hope you're well. I've always wondered how you are. I'd like to see you—I just hope you'll come. Bye, then."

Gabe listens to the message again. He puts the phone down. He swore when he left home that he'd never go back, not for anything. Now George is telling him that Jonah has stopped drinking. Isn't that wonderful? Gabe drinks enough for the both of them at this point, and he can't see George in his current state, or ever. And what the hell is George doing hanging around with Jonah anyway? Nothing makes any sense. *You're drunk. Didn't happen.* He picks up the bottle again. He drinks almost all of it in an endless gulp that makes his throat and chest feel like they've been filled with gasoline, then ignited. He pours the rest of the bourbon over the phone and watches the screen go black. A few minutes later, he passes out.

Watch the rain fall on the river from the screened-in porch.

The last time George looked Jonah in the eye was thirty years ago, after Virginia died. Jonah had come to the door of the inn and banged hard.

"He killed her!" Jonah had shouted, over and over, when George answered.

"Be quiet!" George said. "Calm down, right now! My wife is sleeping." She had not slept for days, and finally, she was out. It was precious, this sleep, and he couldn't allow Jonah to interrupt it. He led Jonah out to the porch, closed the door behind them. "Now, what are you talking about?"

"Gabe killed her. My boy. He killed them both," Jonah said, and then he had told George a tale that had no merit, that disgusted George even now when he thought about it, that a grown man could blame a child for an accident, when it was Jonah's fault, or no one's. Or when it was George's fault alone. He shook with anger, and he shook with shame.

When Jonah was finished, George composed himself and said, "I'm taking him. I'm taking Gabriel away from you, Jonah. I'm going to the cabin in my boat right now, and I'm getting him and I'm bringing him here, and this is where he's going to live." Never in his life had he been so prepared to hurt another person. He doesn't like to think about what he would have done if Jonah had fought him on it. He didn't consult with Lilly on this decision; he didn't have to. He knew she'd agree because there were only so many times you could see a little boy bruised the way Gabe was sometimes bruised, and know it was happening at the hands of a father who drank too much to know better, or perhaps had never known better, and not do a damn thing about it. Maybe if someone had saved Jonah from his own abusive drunkard of a father years before, things would have been different. But they weren't different.

Lilly and George spoke of it only briefly, later. He told her what Jonah had said and he told her he wanted them to take Gabe in, for good. She closed her eyes, then opened them and explained the steps... George had been about to leave the room and set about the somewhat complicated business at hand, to add this to the pile of things he never discussed with his wife—another item buried in their graveyard of painful subjects—but found he couldn't.

"How did you know all this, where I would need to go and what I would need to do?"

"Virginia," Lilly said. "In the hospital, before she—she asked me to take care of him. So I asked Viv to look into it for me."

For many years George had been glad to know this. But his guilt surrounding Virginia was not to be so easily pacified. That awful business with Gabe and the money, that sad, confusing night and the days that followed with Gabe gone and Mae heartbroken—all that happened.

George needed to avoid looking at Jonah when he saw him on the street after that, needed to pretend he was no one and especially not the father of the boy they had all believed to be theirs. It worked, somewhat. So long as you didn't get too close to him, you could forget that a man such as Jonah Broadbent existed.

But then, just last week, Jonah walked into town and checked into The Ship. One morning, when George was sitting at Cathy's café drinking his coffee and trying to do the crossword, he saw Jonah shuffle over to a nearby table. George stood to leave, folded up the crossword, threw money on the table, passed Jonah's table with his head held high. Except he couldn't help it: he looked at him. And Jonah's face was different. His eyes were...the only word George could use was *dead*.

"Jonah?" he found himself saying.

"Do I know you, sir?"

"Of course you do. George Summers."

Jonah shook his head. "Sorry. Doesn't sound familiar. Would you like to sit?"

George did sit, and every single person eating breakfast or drinking coffee in that restaurant stared.

"I know you because you knew my—" the word *daughter* halted him "—because you knew Virginia. And also because...because I knew your son quite well. Gabriel. Gabe. He lived with us."

Jonah shook his head. "I'm sorry," he said. "I don't know anyone named Virginia. And I don't have a son."

Jonah was not feigning. George could see that plainly. And he wasn't drunk either. He was just lost.

"Would you like a saltine?" Jonah asked. "I always ask for extra, but I got a few too many and I don't want to waste them." Jonah's hand shook badly as he passed George the little packet.

"Thank you." George took one out, chewed, swallowed. He tried to think of what to say next, but in the end, it didn't matter. Jonah seemed happy just to have him sitting there.

"See you tomorrow?" he asked a little later, his voice full of hope.

"See you tomorrow."

The next day at Cathy's, Jonah asked, "How long have you lived in Alex Bay?"

"My whole life," George said. "You?"

"Awhile." That blank, vulnerable look.

"I think you might need a doctor. Can I take you to the doctor?"

Jonah shook his head. "No. Don't need a doctor. Don't have any money."

"You were in Vietnam."

"Wasn't in Nam."

"Yes, Jonah. You were. So you should have some veteran's benefits. I can help you with that."

The waitress came over with a fresh pot of coffee and more saltines. They sat in silence and George thought about how angry Lilly would be at him right now if she could see him sitting here with Jonah. And, if the rumor mill was as well oiled as it always had been in this town, she'd know about it soon enough. "Let's go see a doctor," he said again, gently.

"No," Jonah replied. "No doctor."

George thought about Gabe, too. Impossible to make anything up to the boy from such a great distance of time. But it felt like he was trying.

It was a few days later when Jonah took the phone number out of his pocket. He said, "You mentioned that I had a son the other day. And I said I didn't, but the thing is—I have this." He unfolded the piece of paper and handed it to George. "I used a computer at the library, and I found it on a website. He does art of some kind—do you remember, those comic books he would make? His number was there, and a picture of him, too. The librarian helped me find it. Him. Who you said. Gabe."

Jonah's hands were especially shaky that day as he put the slip of paper back in his breast pocket. George walked him back to The Ship later, and helped him to his room, where Jonah lay on the bed and almost immediately fell asleep while George stood in the door frame, not sure what to do.

He walked over to the bed and looked down at Jonah. And in a move so fast it felt like a reflex, he reached into Jonah's breast pocket and took out that piece of paper. It wasn't his to take. But Lilly's keepsake box hadn't been his to take either. When the paper was in his hand, he felt there was nothing else to do but shove it in his pocket and leave the room

Except there was something else to do. George called Gabe. He heard the boy's voice. He asked him to come back. He asked him to come home because it was what *he* wanted, and he didn't think about how Lilly was going to feel. And that felt damn good.

Plan what you'll do on your next trip here.

You'll be back.

This place has a magnetic pull.

You'll see.

"Mae, we have confirmation that Bradley was on a flight to Cape Town Tuesday night. But the South African authorities then lost track of him." In the distance, Mae hears a phone ring, car horns honking outside, someone coughing. There is a bag at her feet. The landlord came back to the apartment and said it was the last time he was asking. Mae didn't have the money and this time she admitted it. He told her she had to get out. He said she could have a few hours. She took her wedding dress out of the closet, crumpled it into a ball, shoved it into the bottom of a duffel bag. She packed some other clothes, she packed her mother's list, she took the dog and some food for him, and she left.

"Did he ever mention South Africa? Do you know if he has any connections there?"

"It's where he said he wanted to go on our honeymoon," she says. "He was doing a lot of research on it. He said he wanted to find somewhere very remote. Somewhere we could hide away. Then I found this island, Tristan da Cunha. He said he was going to book it once a few checks came in. Maybe that's where he was heading. To the place we were supposed to go on our goddamn honeymoon." She laughs, a bitter sound. The looks of pity on their faces are making her sick again. "Look, I can't keep coming back here. I have to go home. Okay? This is too much, this is more than a human being should be expected to take." Her voice is rising, she can hear her anger rather than feel it because all she feels right now is numb. "I've literally told you everything I know about him, and it's not much and I need a break. Let me answer questions by phone or something if you need more from me. But, really, enough is enough!"

They tell her to calm down. They tell her the case is about to be transferred to the FBI; they tell her they won't need her again until he's found, *if* he's found, if there's a trial. They tell her she's free to go, but they don't ask her where she's going and she wishes they had. She would have apologized for shouting at them, she would have thanked them for trying to find him, for at least trying to get the money back for the people who lost it so unwittingly, and she would have told them about the islands, about the legends and lore of her town, about Pirate Bill, about the invention of Thousand Island dressing, about the ghosts, about her dreams.

She would have told them that she was someone else, that there was more to her than this life they had caught a glimpse of, that this was not her, none of it was.

Except she wasn't sure she believed that anymore.

So instead, she wrote down her grandparents' phone number and address, and she left.

Bud slumps on the sidewalk, taking up so much space that people trying to walk past glare at her. Her phone battery is dying, and she left her charger in the apartment. The landlord has changed the locks already; she wishes she hadn't checked. She stares at the screen for a moment, thinking about whom she could call before it dies. Her grandparents? No. Better just to explain everything, or try to, when she gets home. A friend? But who? All her new friends want an explanation she can't give, and all her old friends haven't heard from her in too long. She can't call anyone and burden them with this. It's hers to carry, alone.

She stands. Bud walks beside her slowly, stopping to look up at her every few paces. "Everything is going to be fine," she says. He presses his nose against her leg and she pats his head, pulls him along until they reach a pawnshop. Its front window is filled with jewelry, musical instruments, car stereos. She pushes open the door.

"You can't bring that dog in here," says a male voice, raspy.

Mae backs out and ties Bud to a parking meter, says, "I'll be right back. Promise."

"What can I do you for?" The man behind the counter is fat and red faced with small yellow teeth.

Mae puts her hand on the counter. She's been putting the ring on every day for fear of losing the only thing she has of any value. "It's a carat and a half yellow diamond, plus the little ones around it, in a platinum setting."

The man lifts up her hand, flops it back and forth, peers at the stone. His fingers are warm and damp.

"Eight hundred bucks."

"Come on! It's worth way more than that."

He laughs. "Darlin', that there is no yellow diamond. It's a yellow *topaz*. Which is worth a helluva lot less."

"But...those *are* diamonds around the—" she grits her teeth against this new information "—topaz, aren't they? Please tell me those are real at least."

"They're real, all right. Real crappy diamonds."

She takes the ring off and clenches her fist around it. She needs money if she's going to take the train to Syracuse and then a long taxi ride since Bud won't be allowed on the bus.

She hasn't driven in so long her license has expired. Peter always drove. "Fifteen hundred."

"Not a chance."

"Thirteen hundred."

"Nope."

"Fine. Forget it." She turns to go.

"Offer stands for eight hundred!" he calls after her. "Your only other option is to keep it on account of the sentimental value. No one will offer you more."

She returns to the cash register. He opens it, counts out the money, hands it to her.

On the train, she sits beside a window and looks outside as it gathers speed. She worries about Bud in the baggage compartment, worries about what George will say at the sight of him. Her grandfather hates dogs. Something about the war. Will he make her take Bud to a shelter? It doesn't seem like something George would do, but she worries about it anyway.

In the seat in front of her a young woman is talking on her cell phone. "Yeah, I'm heading home for a few days. Going to spend some time with the parents before they completely lose it." The girl laughs and Mae tries not to hate a person she's never met simply because she doesn't understand how easy it is to lose people. Mae watches the city lights spooling out and then fading away. Then the city is gone. *I'm going to see the river*, she imagines herself saying into her cell phone, to some best friend she doesn't have. *I'm going to see my family.* And at least there is that: Lilly and George, older and slower but still a reassuring presence in her life, still constant, still something she can believe in.

She presses her cheek against the glass and waits for the river to materialize beside her like a ghost. Instead, she sees memories out there in the cold: a snowy hill in a farmer's field. And there she and Gabe are again, riding their toboggans down that slope, hitting frozen cabbage roots and flying off their sleds, laughing through mouthfuls of snow, not caring about the bruises, not caring about what hurt. And she sees her mother, too, with her long red-gold hair and her blue-green eyes and her ivory skin and the freckles across the bridge of her nose. Her mother was a rainbow of colors Mae had never seen before, and has never seen again. Her mother was younger than Mae is now when she died.

What would she want me to do?

Brave. She would want me to be brave. Mae has very few memories of Virginia that she is certain she didn't cobble together out of wishes, but there is one that has always felt solid: a trip she took with Gabe and her parents the summer before Virginia and Chase died. The four of them drove across the border into Canada on their way to a cabin in the Laurentian Mountains. Why did they go away in the middle of the summer, in the middle of the high season? Mae has never asked. The cabin was magic, it was up on stilts, it overlooked the Rouge River, it was made entirely of logs with little decks off every bedroom. "It can be just like this, different from any of the other cabins on *any* of the other islands" Mae heard her mother say to her father. She realized they were dreaming of building their own structure: a fishing camp on the island they owned.

The four of them canoed and fished every day on a river that was smaller, colder and calmer than the one Mae was used to. There weren't any islands she could see. They had picnics on the riverbank in the afternoons and one day friends came to visit and Virginia made a shore lunch under a hazy blue sky. There was a light breeze to keep the bugs away, there were river-caught fish sizzling over cedar logs, there were brown beans and bacon, potatoes and onions, canned peaches, coffee for the grown-ups and apple cider for Gabe and Mae.

Later, Virginia took Mae and Gabe with her into town to buy groceries and drop their garbage at the dump. Her father was sleeping: had he been drinking? Mae doesn't remember and tells herself he wasn't, that it was a perfect week. Mae and Gabe sat in the car while Virginia unloaded the bags from the trunk. The two of them were talking about moose be-cause they had seen one on the opposite bank earlier in the day and Mae's dad had said to be careful around moose: they charged. "What would you do if you saw one and it looked like it was going to charge at you?" Gabe asked her. Mae said play dead, Gabe said climb a tree—and then Gabe looked out the window and said, "Woah. See that? Imagine one of *those* charged at you."

Mae climbed into the front seat and squinted out. *"Woah."* But Virginia just kept pulling the black bags out of the trunk, walking to the edge of the pit, throwing them in. Once, one of the bears looked up at her and Mae almost screamed.

"I should tell her to get in here," Mae said. But she was paralyzed, she couldn't move even to save her mother from the bears she obviously, somehow, was *not* seeing. Virginia dropped the last bag in and stood still, one hand held up, shielding her eyes while she stared into the pit at all those bears clustered around the garbage heap like a big family. She turned and saw Gabe and Mae watching her, and she grinned at them, walked over to the car, opened the door. "Want a closer look?"

"No way! What if they *eat* us? Mama, are you crazy?"

"They're way too far away, down at the bottom there, with plenty of delicious garbage to keep them busy. And even if they did decide they were more interested in us, they'd never get anywhere close before we made it back to the car." Mae's eyes widened and Virginia laughed. "And they're not going to come running over here, Mae-bell. They're not interested in us."

"I saw one of them look at you."

"Sure, he was just checking me out, making sure I wasn't a more delicious dining option than a half-full can of Beef-aroni."

"But what if they decide we *do* look delicious?"

"Then I'll save you. I'll get you into the car."

"But what if you can't save us, what if we can't run fast enough?"

"Sometimes when you're afraid, you just have to do the thing that scares you most. That's just what you have to do. Okay?"

But Mae couldn't do it. She watched through the windshield, sweat trickling down her back and slicking her palms, as her mother led Gabe to the edge of the pit. She remembers he high-fived her when he got back in the car, said it was *rad*, his new Gabe word. She remembers feeling regret and wishing to be as brave as her mother was, as he was. But it turned out Gabe wasn't so brave after all. And now, try as she does, she can never manage to extract him from her favorite childhood memories. She can forget Peter, she already knows this, she's doing it now in small, raw increments. But letting go of Gabe would mean forgetting she ever had a childhood. It would mean forgetting her brave, beautiful mother, the imperfect father who loved her. And she can't do that. Mae stares into the darkness, looking for lost people until she falls asleep. It's dreamless. She's alone.

Legend has it that the Iroquois used to go down to the shores of the bay in the spring to bathe in the water because they believed it would cure them of all their winter ailments—especially when it was raining.

So go swimming in the rain!

Why not?

You're already wet. (My mother is making me add that you are not allowed to go swimming if there is thunder and lightning. I feel like everyone knows that.)

Lilly has seen marriages fall apart before, but she never imagined her own would. Especially not at this late juncture, after sixty-seven years of marriage—an unimaginably long time, even now, looking back at it. Aren't the twilight years the point during which you're supposed to go gently into that good night, holding the hand of your partner? Isn't this why people stay together at all, through thick and thin, through high and low, instead of packing it in around midlife, when desire and tolerance wane at the same time? Not that that happened with George. Really, they hadn't had that many lows, not relationshipwise, anyway. Life lows, sure: into their lives, rain had certainly fallen, and they had had to weather the storms. But they had done so together. Until now.

Should she have argued, begged him to stay? Perhaps. If there was one thing she had learned about marriage it was that you had to choose wisely which hills you were going to die upon, and she was in absolutely no shape right now to do battle. *I'm losing something*, she should have said to him. *My memory, I think. My mind. My grasp. On everything. Sometimes, I forget who I am.* A terrifying truth, and she thinks it would devastate George more than it is devastating her. *But I do love you, George. I do.*

"He's still living in a room at The Ship?"

Lilly comes around from her reverie. "Yes," she says. Where is she? Ah, by the river. And who is this? Vivian: her best friend, her oldest friend, the friend who knows everything, almost. We all need one of those, a friend who can go away and come back, or we can go away from and come back to, and it will be like nothing has changed—although these friends are to be expected to say the things we don't want to hear. We cannot be upset when they do. Vivian is Everett's sister, so she knows more than anyone. She will circle around the truth and then close in, eventually. Vivian always does.

"Are you all right?"

"I'm fine. Don't worry about me." Today is one of her good days, so it's not exactly a lie. "Yes, it stings that he's gone, but I'm sure in another day or two George will be back and we'll sort it out."

"Do you believe that?"

"I have to."

"Have you tried going to fetch him?"

"No, I have not. Too stubborn, I guess. But I've considered it."

"You've been a good wife. You don't deserve this."

This support from her comrade brings sudden tears to Lilly's eyes. She blinks and walks faster.

"Foolish man," Vivian continues, catching up. "You see, this is why I could never stay married for long."

Lilly laughs, feels grateful to be able to laugh, still. "Oh, is that why? I always thought you didn't stay married for long because you married such dolts."

Vivian laughs, too.

And then, just as swift as the laughter came, she's on to the next feeling. It's all she can do to keep walking, not turn and bury her face in her friend's shoulder and let the tears fall. "Thank you" is all she says. "For understanding."

"I'm worried about you. It's not just this situation with George that—"

"I said I'm *fine.*"

"You'd better call Dr. Carroll," Vivian says.

"I already have. I've been referred to a specialist. Dr. Turnbull—I know him well, from volunteering at the hospital, so at least it won't be a stranger I'll be seeing."

"And you'll go to the appointment?"

"Of course I will. But don't say anything. I haven't told George. Not yet. Not now."

"Fair enough." They cross the street and carefully take the stairs down to the river viewing platform. It's their destination during every one of their walks. There's a light shining on one of the islands: Jonah Broadbent's, Island 51; Lilly knows that without hardly even looking. She stands still, and the snowflakes continue to fall on her cap of silver-white hair. At the salon every month they give her a special rinse: it's violet when they put it on but it turns her hair vivid white when they're done. "You have such beautiful white hair," the stylist says every time, and Lilly feels a little vain about it. Imagine feeling vain about white hair.

"I need to tell you something. You didn't come to bridge this week, so you didn't hear the news."

"What is it?"

"It's about Jonah Broadbent."

"I can't imagine why I'd care about anything to do with Jonah Broadbent."

"Well, you might care about this. Checked himself into The Ship motel. He was spotted eating meals at Coffee Pot Cathy's and the North Star. He had coffee with his meals, not booze, and never goes into the tavern or the Legion. He's even kind to the waitresses."

"He's stopped drinking again, terrific!" Sarcasm doesn't come easily to Lilly, and she doesn't like how much spite there is in her words. "What does it matter now?" she says in a quieter voice.

"He was seen eating with George. More than once."

"You're sure? He was eating with George and not some other obstinate old man?" The spite is back; it never went anywhere in the first place.

"It was him. I saw them, too. I was trying to figure out how to tell you. I thought it would be best over an afternoon glass of sherry. But now—Martha said she heard George found him unconscious in his room yesterday. Jonah isn't well. He's in the hospital."

Lilly keeps staring out at the light on the island. "George used to tell me everything," she says.

"They think it was a stroke. Severe. Memory loss accompanied it, so he might have had a few beforehand."

This makes Lilly think. Is this what's going on with her? She'd know if she'd had a stroke, wouldn't she? Surely she knows herself better than someone who drank himself into oblivion every day for more than fifty years?

"I wonder if Gabriel knows about this," Lilly says, instead of voicing her frightened thoughts.

"There's a light on at Jonah's place."

Lilly breathes out sharply, a puff of cold white. Could it be?

"That boy was your family once," Vivian continues. There she is, circling the truth.

"He was." She has the sudden urge to confess to Vivian, as if what happened with George has opened floodgates and all secrets must now come out, before she forgets what they are.

"He was a good boy, at heart."

"Yes," Lilly says. "I think I should get back home now. See if maybe George has had a change of heart and come home."

Later, when she is alone in her silent house, she washes the dishes from the day and stares out at the river. She wishes for spring. She wishes she could swim in the river and feel cleansed, wishes she could engage in her secret ritual. Nothing much, just an annual springtime swim, but why had she never shared it with her daughter? She never told Virginia about the magic in the river when her daughter was alive, instead focusing on the wrong things—constant corrections, judgments, many of which still hang, though they're hidden, in her daughter's "Things to Do When It's Raining" list in the lobby, a yellowing monument to the life that once made this place bright. Maybe the magic in the river will remain a secret, too. And that's okay, because some things are better kept secret. And some things are not: life's most difficult task is to know which is which.

Alex Bay is not always the most exciting town in the world. (My mother says she wishes I would cross that out.)

If it's raining and you're getting bored, take the train to a nearby town.

A change of scene might do you good.

The movement of the train has lulled Gabe to sleep. Is it a dream? Is it a memory? Is there a difference? Grade one. Mae was his best friend. The kids at school thought it was weird that his best friend was a girl in kindergarten, but Gabe didn't care. Mae was the most wonderful person in the world, other than her mother, Virginia, and her grandparents, Lilly and George. Gabe wasn't quite as certain about Chase, Virginia's husband. Chase would lift Mae up, spin her around, tickle her until she was gasping with laughter—but sometimes, when Gabe was sure Chase thought he wasn't looking, he saw a darkness in Chase's eyes that reminded him of his own father's darkness. He didn't want someone like Chase around Mae. He feels guilty now, even remembering these thoughts.

Mae didn't play with dolls. She played outside, like him. What she loved most was to swim in the river, and this was how they first met, in town, at the beach. He was jumping off the pier, over and over, by himself, and then she was beside him, jackknifing and cannonballing, too.

"Keep your eyes open, and I will, too, and we'll jump and see who sinks down farthest," she said. He didn't want to admit he was scared, that he had never opened his eyes in the river underwater because the way his dad talked about muskie fish made him imagine them lurking everywhere, ready to bite if you made eye contact. But he did it. He didn't want her to think he was a coward. And he didn't see any fish: he saw only her eyes, wide and full of light even in the depths of the river. He stared into them until she squeezed them shut, grabbed his hands, pulled him to the surface along with her.

She said to him at the end of that day, "We have a rope and it swings out over the water. You should come to my house and try it." This was his luckiest, luckiest moment.

Soon, Gabe was playing at Mae's house almost every day. There were some days when Jonah said no, he wouldn't ferry him across the river in his boat. *Fuck off, go away, swim if you want to go so bad.* Gabe was seven, almost eight. This year, he was going to learn how to drive the boat himself and then he'd be free to do what he liked. When his father pulled the boat up to the dock at the inn, Mae always ran down to greet him, and studiously ignored Jonah.

"You know," Jonah said to her one day, and Gabe felt afraid—normally, Jonah didn't talk to people, and especially not to kids. "I'm friends with your mama. Or, at least, I used to be." Mae wrinkled her nose and looked up at him. His father was not nice to look at: too skinny, but with a pot-belly. A dirty undershirt, a red face, hair that looked like it was buzzed off regularly by a lawnmower, a cigarette hanging from his downturned lips, yellow-stained fingers. Was it true, that his father was friends with Mae's mother? Her mother was beautiful, beautiful like Mae but more beautiful, even. Virginia's hair was red and her eyes were blue-green and she had the best smile, a smile that seemed made only for the person she was smiling at. Also, she was really good at fishing. Like, really, *really* good.

"Who do you think taught your mom to fish the way she

does?" Jonah asked Mae, before turning the motor on again and puttering away from them.

Mae watched him go. "He's lying," Gabe said.

She grabbed Gabe's arm and peered down at his burn mark, the one that had appeared a few days before, round and angry red, the shape of one of Jonah's cigarettes "It's getting better," she said. "We don't need the ointment today. Come on, let's go play."

Most of the games they played had to do with imagining things. Gabe could sometimes imagine himself right out of his own reality. He imagined he lived at the inn, that Mae was his sister. Except not his sister, no—he wanted Mae to be something else, just he didn't know what. Not yet.

It got better for Gabe when school started, because then his father had to give him a ride across the river in the boat every day or he'd get another visit from the authorities. Had Mac's family said something? He didn't know. They'd never bothered with him before, but now people seemed to care whether he went to school. After school, Gabe walked over to the inn with Mae. They swam until it got too late in the season. They ate spaghetti, and macaroni and cheese, and pork chops fried in a pan, and ice cream out of little metal dishes like the ones you got in the restaurants Gabe had never been to.

They played in the attic of Summers' Inn or in Mae's room. On weekends, sometimes he would even sleep over. Those were the best nights, because he didn't have that tight feeling in his chest as the time approached when he knew he needed to go home. He would sleep in a sleeping bag on Mae's bed and Virginia would come in and sing to them, the same song every time. It made him feel jealous for the first time in his life, a deep pang in his stomach. His own mom had left when he was three. Jonah never mentioned her and got angry when Gabe asked.

On the nights he didn't get to stay over, Virginia would take Gabe home in her boat. They would ride across the river and Virginia would ask him questions about his day like he was her friend, not just some kid. And one night, he finally worked up the courage to say to her, "If you and my dad are friends, or used to be friends, how come you never talk to him?"

Virginia gave him a long look and he couldn't interpret it and hoped he hadn't said something bad that would mean he would not be allowed to play with Mae anymore.

"Did your dad tell you we were friends?"

He nodded.

"Well, yes, it's true. I've known him for a long time. Since we were kids, like you and Mae." She turned off the boat and tied it to the dock, her fingers moving like lightning. "He was my best friend once. Like you and Mae. Two peas in a pod. I hated playing with girls. Your daddy liked to fish with me. He didn't mind touching worms. So we did that together, almost every day."

His mouth dropped open. "Really?"

"Really. We had a lot of good times." A smile played across her lips and he could see that she was remembering things, good things, about his father. It was inconceivable, and yet here it was. "Maybe I should pay him a visit," she said.

Gabe prayed, hard and silent, that his father wasn't drunk. Out of nowhere, he thought, *Mae cannot know about this.*

"Your son told me to come up and say hello."

There was a beat of silence. But then Jonah replied in an unfamiliar voice. A friendly voice. Maybe even a happy voice. "He did, did he? And here I was just brewing up some coffee. Nice and strong, the way you like it, Gigi. Want some?"

Gigi? Gabe pretended to play in the sand while they sat on the dock and talked. The sun was about to set and Virginia was going to have to turn on her boat light to get home. Eventually, they got up and left their empty cups on the dock and Jonah took Virginia to see the hovercraft he'd been rebuilding—*they'd* been rebuilding, because Jonah made Gabe help, told him he'd better make himself useful or else, even if he was just a snot-nosed first grader. Gabe hated being in his father's messy old shed, helping him fix boats—but he loved driving them, and Jonah had said if he helped enough, he'd let him drive whenever he wanted, maybe even give him his own boat to fix up. Jonah was planning to sell the hovercraft once he got it fixed up. It was how he made money: salvaging old boats and selling them, except he never seemed to do it right and a lot of times the people complained, and Jonah blamed Gabe, and Gabe wanted to cry, but what else was new?

"I could use this," Virginia said. "Chase and I are working on building a fishing camp and log cabin on our island. Next year, we're going to start our own business: fishing trips and shore lunches. Like a bed and breakfast, but fishing and lunch." She grinned, and so did Jonah. "I wanted to have the structure finished before winter, but unless we have a way to cross the new ice, I don't think we will. This would be perfect. How soon do you think you'll have this rebuilt?"

"Lickety-split," Jonah said.

Lickety-split. Jonah never used words like that.

Virginia smiled. "Hey, you should work for us," she said. "Next season, as a guide. Everyone knows you're the second-best muskie angler in Alex Bay."

"Second best, huh? I taught you everything you know, girl."

Gabe imagined his father working for Virginia and Chase, actually having a job, getting up mornings and going out and coming back like all the other fathers at school, and he felt excited. But he also felt nervous. Two words he wanted to say to her: *be careful.* Instead, he took their coffee cups and washed them carefully in the sink. Then he got a perma- nent marker and put an *X* on the bottom of the one Virginia had used, so he'd never forget that she'd been there, and had taught him something about his father that he had not known to be true before.

Gabe opens his eyes. Syracuse. He can feel the train gearing up again. Just in time, he grabs his backpack, hurries down the steps of the train and walks into the night as quickly as he can, before he changes his mind, before he decides to just lie down in a snowbank or something, to die rather than get on the bus that will take him home.

Read a mystery novel, all in one sitting.

What is that sound? Who is it... George?

The telephone.

Lilly opens her eyes, sits up, *ring, ring, ring*, and at this time of night, a ringing phone can mean only one thing. Pain in her chest, pain in her heart, "Hello?"

Silence. Breathing. "Who's there? Make yourself known!"

"It's Peter."

"Peter? I don't know anyone named Peter."

"Please, Lilly. I don't have much time. Is Mae there?"

"Mae *here*? Why would she be here? She's in the city. That's where she lives."

"Oh. She didn't...? I was sure she'd go home—sorry. Really, I'm sorry." There's a click and then the dial tone and Lilly is sure for a moment that she's going to have a heart attack. But she stands up and doesn't fall over dead, so she leaves the bedroom and goes downstairs to her desk. With George gone there's no reason not to flip the lights on as she goes, so she makes it to her desk easily, and opens her navy leather address book when she gets there. She finds Mae's cell phone number, dials and feels hope and relief when she hears Mae's voice right away, but then the hope falls away because the voice is telling her to *leave a message and I'll call you back as soon as possible.* Lilly hangs up, dials again, same result. "It's your grandmother," she says. "Please call home. Someone was looking for you and he sounded like bad news, and I'm worried."

She hangs up again and stares down at the...the...

Telephone.

If there is any right moment to call George this is the one, but to her horror she can no longer remember where he went.

He's staying at, he went to, he said he was...

She stands in the lobby, alone in her white nightgown, and cries like an overgrown child. Peter called, on the *telephone.* Peter—she remembers now, Mae's Peter, but Mae isn't here, and she doesn't know why that is either. She doesn't know where either of them went and she doesn't know when they're coming home.

The biggest muskies always come out when it rains.

Best bait ever: large safety pin with tinsel attached.

The fishermen call this the Virginia Summers, just so

you know.

I'm pretty good at fishing.

There are lights on upstairs and in the lobby. But when Mae taps at the door, no one comes. She knocks again. Then the door opens and her grandmother is there, looking alarmed and confused but also achingly, wonderfully familiar with her white cap of hair and her long flannel nightgown. "Mae! You came!"

Mae steps inside, pulling Bud by the collar. She closes the door against the blowing snow. The dog is dripping dirty slush onto the threadbare carpet but sitting very straight and still, as if he were trying to make the best possible impression regardless.

"What on earth?"

"He's—Peter's dog."

"How did you get here? Where's Peter?" Lilly leans her head around Mae to peer out the window. Then she puts her hand to her forehead. "He called here before. He was looking for you..."

Mae looks alarmed. "He did? Are you sure?"

"No," Lilly says. "No, I'm not sure, actually."

"Are you okay?"

"No," Lilly says again.

"Grandma, what's wrong? Where's Grandpa? Are you sick?"

Too much silence, but then, "I'm fine," Lilly says, with force. "I'm fine now. Take off your things. Let's go into the kitchen." She turns and walks ahead, turning off lights as she goes. Her nightgown shines like a beacon ahead of Mae in the darkness of the hall, but the kitchen is bright. Bud follows behind her.

Mae tries again. "Is Grandpa upstairs, asleep?"

"I told you, no. He's away. Would you like some brandy? I think this is a night for brandy."

"Away? But where?"

Lilly pours brandy, pulls out two chairs. "You tell me what happened. Don't worry about anything else right now."

"Peter and I broke up." Mae sees relief pass over her grandmother's face, quickly, like a cloud passing over the sun on a windy day.

"Another woman?"

"Worse."

"Another *man*?"

Mae laughs for a surprising moment—when was the last time she laughed? She takes a gulp of brandy, then explains about the Ponzi scheme, the police, WindSpan Turbine never existing. "I'm sorry," she says when the entire mess has spilled out of her. "I'm so sorry. He took your money, everyone's money. And it's my fault."

"Your fault?"

"I should have known. I should have done something."

Lilly is petting Bud's neck absently, as if he has always been there at her feet. "Well," she says. "I suppose I always had a feeling about him. That he wasn't quite all he seemed to be. Bit of a show pony, really. But sometimes we see what we want to see in a person…" She trails off and looks down at Bud as if she's now surprised to find him there.

"Are you mad? About the money?"

"I'd be lying if I said I wasn't disappointed. But it wasn't everything we had. And maybe they'll find him, and everyone will get their money back."

"Maybe."

Lilly stands and takes their empty glasses to the sink. Mae can hear George's voice in her mind. *Everything in moderation.* If you were going to drink liquor, only one, no matter the gravity of the situation.

"Where's Grandpa?"

Her grandmother is motionless for a moment, staring out the window. She looks smaller than she did even a month before.

"He's away right now." Lilly's tone is remote.

"Where did he go?"

"Oh…just away."

"Grandma. Please."

She turns. "We had a disagreement," she says. "And he went away for a little while, to clear his head, I suppose. He's staying at a hotel."

"I— He *what?* Which hotel?"

Lilly pauses for a moment. Is it possible she doesn't know which hotel? But then she exclaims, "The Ship!" and smiles. Her dentures look too big for her mouth suddenly, her expression too joyous in relation to the news she has just delivered. Mae has to look away, when she knows she should do something else, hug her grandmother, say she's sorry, say she's sure George will be back soon. But it's preposterous, what Lilly has just said. The idea of her grandfather gone at all is too shocking for her to begin to understand, never mind know how to comfort Lilly about.

"He hates The Ship" is all Mae manages. "He hates all hotels, except for this one."

"People change their minds about things," Lilly replies. "It just happens. You can't stay sure about everything your whole life." Her words are clipped and matter-of-fact. She's her pragmatic self once more. "Now, let's go up to bed. I'm sure you're exhausted from your journey."

Mae isn't; she slept on the train. But she follows Lilly up the stairs, and Bud trails Lilly as if he's forgotten all about Mae. Lilly gets fresh sheets and hands them to Mae. "Perhaps your dog would like to sleep in *my* room," she says, and there's that smile again, but Mae forces herself to meet it head-on. "Your grandfather would hate that. But he's not here, is he?" Mae gets that sensation again, the idea that Lilly is searching for something. An answer. *Is he?* She reaches for her grandmother, hugs her tight, squeezes her eyes closed against the reality of her birdlike bones.

"Good night, dear." The door to her grandparents' room closes before Mae can see inside. She doesn't like the feeling upstairs, the emptiness. Someone is missing, another person is gone from this house. And it's her grandfather, the most reliable man she's ever known.

She makes her bed, finds an old T-shirt in one of her drawers to sleep in and lies down. She didn't close the curtains and the moon is full. It reminds her of a big flashlight, up there in the sky—and flashlights remind her of Gabe, who used to sneak into this room with one when they were kids. After her parents died he started to live at the inn, almost. It felt like a special gift, like a surprise for Mae. But he was like a visitor from a foreign land, maybe even another world; periodically, he'd go back to the cabin for a day or two, and she never knew when that would be. Then he'd appear at the inn again, a pilgrim returned. Mae asked him hundreds of times why he couldn't just stay, couldn't just belong to *them*, but he would never answer. Perhaps she should have seen it coming, then. She should have known he was never going to be hers.

He'd creep in late at night, carrying his little flashlight and some book or other, usually a joke book. He was a better reader than she was, and not just because he was older: Gabe was smart. They would make a tent with her duvet, his head the highest point, and he would hold a flashlight and read to her. Jokes if she was extra sad and missing her parents—"Where do cows go on a date?"

"The moooo-vies."

"What kind of cheese isn't yours?"

"Nacho cheese!"—and she would always laugh, even if she had heard the joke dozens of times before. Or, if she wasn't in need of too much cheering up, they would tell each other stories about the Boldt Castle widower haunting the shore, or the spirits of priests that lived on the Isle of Pines that everyone in town knew about, which made them a town of believers in ghosts. Then they'd lie beside each other in silence, listening to the sounds the old inn made in the middle of the night: clicking radiators, dripping faucets, clanging pipes and a gentle sighing Mae always wondered if she was imagining, an ancient sound from within the walls that made her feel the place was alive, not a structure but a being, a member of the family, another ghost beside a river that teemed with them.

One night, she started to sing Gabe the song her mother always used to sing to get her to sleep. "Your Grandpa would sing this to me," Virginia would whisper to Mae. Gabe reached for her hand and held it in the darkness. "I love that song," he said. She didn't know what it was called because no one had ever told her, but it was about a sly old gentleman who lived on Featherbed Lane.

"I like that part about the dreams," Gabe whispered.

"You're my best friend," she told him. "And we're always going to be best friends, no matter what. Promise?"

"Swear to God."

"But you don't believe in God. Swear to Han Solo."

"I swear to Han Solo, we will always be best friends."

They woke the next morning to find that the blankets had been tucked around them. Lilly never said anything when she found Gabe in Mae's room. At least not back then.

Mae opens her eyes. Damask wallpaper, toile curtains, knotty pine furniture and a dog now in bed with her; Bud must have found her in the night. She looks at the digital clock on the bedside table, the one she's had since grade six, gray and pink with turquoise squiggles on white plastic. It says 8:15. Bud pushes his snout into one of her hips. She hits the snooze button and sits up.

"Bud, okay, okay. Listen, though. Lilly was nice to you last night, but you're on probation." She stands, pulls on some old jeans. Bud dials down the exuberance of his tail wagging, then walks sedately down the hall, hitting a Royal Doulton dancing figurine; Mae catches it just in time and puts it back on the table, to dance pointlessly once more.

Her grandmother has left the pot full of coffee and a note on the kitchen table saying she's gone into town for some groceries. Mae looks out the window and sees the fresh tire tracks.

Bud is whining, nudging at her hip. She moves toward the front vestibule and finds an old pair of winter boots in the closet. Outside, Bud stands beside her, ears pushed forward, head cocked. She takes him down the drive and then turns toward the river, where they're met with a blast of wind.

At the river, she unclips Bud's leash and he runs out onto the ice immediately. "Bud, wait!" She knows the ice is sound, at least a foot thick at this point in a cold winter. Still, she doesn't have the courage to go out onto the ice; she hasn't since her parents died. She stands on the bank and tries not to picture Bud plunging through.

Farther out on the river, movement. She lifts her hand to shield her eyes from the sun. A man is walking across the ice. It looks like he's coming from Island 51, or at least from that direction. No one else but Jonah is crazy enough to live on an island on the river year-round. And he's not a fisherman; he doesn't have any gear. A black tuque is pulled down over his ears. Mae's heart starts pounding. Fast.

She has feared Gabe's father, silently and viscerally, for as long as she can remember. And now, seeing him out on the ice, she has the urge to run. It's been at least ten years since she last saw him in town, and she crossed the street to avoid him. He's coming closer. "Bud! Come!" Bud tears toward her. She turns and walks the other way, never looking back.

Once she's at the inn, she jiggles the sticky door and reenters the lobby. The smell of wet dog is already taking over. There are familiar things everywhere: the painting of the first Alexandria Bay settlers by the river negotiating with a tribe of Iroquois; the tall bucket of umbrellas; the cuckoo clock (a gift from Dutch guests and silent now; apparently there is no one alive anymore, at least not in the vicinity, with the expertise to fix such a clock); and, there: her mother's "Things to Do When It's Raining" list, tacked to the bulletin board, the same list she has kept a copy of all these years. She steps closer and runs a finger down the list as if that could bring her closer, as if that could bring her mother back to life.

The door opens and Mae drops the page.

Lilly is breathing heavily. "There's a huge bag of dog food in the car; I hope it's the right kind. You'll have to carry it in."

"Of course. I could have gone to get it myself." Instant guilt.

"Not to worry." Bud has trotted over and is wagging his tail at Lilly. She reaches out to pat his head. "Hello, dog."

Mae goes outside and carries the bag into the kitchen.

"Did you have a nice walk with...the dog?" Lilly asks. She's filling the kettle.

"With Bud? Yes. It was *cold*. It's not cold like this in the city. I forgot." Mae pours Bud's food into a chipped bowl that Lilly has produced. Water goes in a Tupperware container. He drinks and sloshes it all over the floor.

Mae makes to rip some paper towel off the roll, but, "Here," says Lilly, handing her a fraying dish towel. Mae has a memory of George hanging paper towels out to dry on the line one summer, when Lilly bought the extra-heavy-duty kind and he insisted they were so absorbent they could be used more than once. They were never wasteful, her grandparents. Because they had lived through a war, George had once explained.

"Are you hungry?" Lilly asks.

"A little. I can make something myself. You don't need to."

But soon there's a plate of toast alongside a little jar of strawberry jam, and her egg sits in a blue cup with a yellow flower on it that has been hers since she was a child.

Mae sits. "I think I saw Jonah Broadbent out on the river this morning..."

Lilly stops, one hand on her hip. "That can't be. Jonah is sick. He's in the hospital. A stroke, Vivian said."

Mae's spoon falls from her fingers and lands with a clunk on the table. If Jonah is sick— But, no. It can't be. There was a time when Mae believed she saw Gabe everywhere, replayed scenes of his return in her mind, and now is not the time to go back there again. Every man walking on the river, every man walking down the street, cannot become a version of Gabe.

"I have my volunteer shift at the hospital this morning,"

Lilly says. For as long as Mae can remember, Lilly has gone to the hospital once a week to sit with elderly people. People who have forgotten who they are, Lilly once said. It seems like a sign to Mae that everything is fine with her grandmother, that whatever she saw in her last night was just because she was tired—and because of George's absence. "I plan to find out what I can about Jonah's condition," Lilly says.

Mae focuses on swallowing, but toast and egg sticks in her throat. "Who cares what happens to Jonah."

In the long silence, Lilly pours her more coffee. "Any plans for the day?"

Still nothing about George, so Mae brings it up. "I was thinking of going to see Grandpa, at The Ship, if that's all right with you."

"No, actually," Lilly says. "No, actually it's not all right with me. I'll tell him you're home. But this is between us, so please don't go there today."

The toast has turned to sawdust in her mouth. She forces it down. "Oh. Okay. If you really don't want me to—"

"I really don't want you to. Thank you. Now, I should go take my bath and get going."

Mae sits at the table until her coffee grows cold. Her grandmother waves on her way out. "We'll order in tonight?" Lilly says cheerfully, as if nothing were amiss. "Just us two girls?"

"Sure," Mae says. More silence, after Lilly is gone. Mae goes upstairs. Bud follows, but continues to wander up and down the hall when she lies on top of her unmade bed. A moment later there's a crash, and Mae knows the girl in the blue dress has danced her last. George would be upset; the figurine was his mother's.

But he isn't here either.

Do something nice for someone else—even just a little thing.

Sometimes on rainy days, people feel sad.

L illy is walking through a set of double doors on her way to the wing where she is to meet Dr. Turnbull for the appointment she had lied about and told Mae was a volunteer shift when the young man swings through the doors; they nearly hit her. A drop of hot coffee lands on her arm. "Oh, shit," he says. "Sorry."

The youth of today. They say things like "Oh, shit" as if it weren't even rude.

But when she looks up, it's not a stranger's face she sees. There's that moment of searching for the name, and then— "Gabriel Broadbent. My goodness. Well, hello." Her heart is racing. Her mind, thank God, is staying where it is.

He has stepped away from her. "Sorry, sorry, I didn't mean to bump into you, and I... Hello, Lilly. How are you?" He has reached the wall and can't get away, though he appears to want to.

"I'm fine, Gabe. How are *you*? I heard about your father. I'm sorry."

Gabe runs his hand through his hair. He could use a good cut, Lilly thinks, and a good shave.

"Yeah. Thanks. Well, I mean, he's not dead." It's impossible to know whether Gabe is happy or sad about this fact.

She steps toward him and pats his shoulder in an awkward gesture she means to be tender, even though she knows she also threw away her right to be tender with him years ago. "I'm so terribly glad to see you," she says. *Terribly*, she thinks. *Terrible.*

Gabe doesn't say anything, but he moves away from the wall. He was always like this, you had to draw him out. Virginia was good at it, Mae was even better.

"You're well?" he asks. "You and George? He called me. But I haven't talked to him. I went to the hotel last night when I got into town, and they told me Jonah was here. So I haven't had a chance… I was just waiting until…"

Lilly tries to smile, cranes her neck to look up at Gabe and pushes the feeling of betrayal down and away. George is not important right now. George is living his own life entirely. "We're fine. Still alive, anyway." Was that the right thing to say? Probably not. But Gabe is staying put.

"And Mae? How is she?"

"Mae is fine. She's…" Lilly clears her throat. Words are stuck there and she isn't sure if she should release them or not. *Gabe, oh, Gabe, I wanted her to be happy so I sent you away. Now she's here and she's so sad and broken.* Instead of this, she says, "She's just fine. Now tell me what's going on with your father. How bad is it?"

"Bad. Very. I've just given them permission to stop the—" He shakes his head.

"It's all right, Gabe. I understand. Where is he?"

"Just down the hall."

"Can I see him?"

"He's not a pretty sight."

"Your father never was."

Gabe chuckles. Lilly remembers him sitting with Mae on the couch, reading jokes to her from a book. Mae would laugh with her mouth open, and he would laugh quietly. Just like this.

Gabe leads her to his father's room and Lilly knows she's going to miss her appointment with Dr. Turnbull, but she doesn't care.

The man in the bed doesn't look like the Jonah she remembers. He resembles a victim of famine. Sunken cheeks, hollow eye sockets, loose skin. Ragged breathing. Jonah but not. Gabe stands beside her, looking down at him. "See?" he says.

A machine beside the bed beeps and Lilly is seized by a sense of urgency. "Come for supper tonight. Come to the inn."

Gabe is silent. Has she made a mistake? Has she come at him too quickly? *Don't forget: you cannot do that with Gabe.*

But then he says, "Maybe I should have done something. They say he had some syndrome, it ate away his brain. From the booze. It killed him, year after year, and no one did any—"

Lilly has to stop him. She can't listen to this. She feels the edges of her memory sharpening. "Gabe, do you think you could give me a moment with him?" she manages.

"Oh. Uh, sure." He backs away.

"Come to the inn," she repeats. "Tonight. For supper. Mae is struggling. She's having some troubles. She could use a friend."

"Okay." He locks eyes with hers. "I'll be in the cafeteria."

When he's gone, she pulls up a chair and sits beside Jonah's bed. She closes her eyes, and when she opens them again, it's Virginia. Her girl. In the hospital bed. Waxy skin and lips tinged blue. Beautiful and fragile, like a sleeping princess.

Virginia is surrounded by machines. There is a blanket on her that seems to breathe: the doctors have explained that it's delivering warm air to her body in careful doses. A rewarm-

ing system, treatment for severe hypothermia. George is getting coffee, Mae is at home with a neighbor. Chase is gone.
Nothing will ever be the same.

Virginia's eyelids flutter, then open. *She's awake! Thank
God, she's awake.* Were her eyes always so big, so beautiful?

Virginia licks her lips, then speaks: "Chase?"

Lilly knows what she's asking, but no. Not yet. "It's me,
Virginia. I'm right here with you."

"How is Mae?"

"She's fine. As well as to be expected. She's at the inn,
with Gabe."

"Promise me that no matter what, you'll always take care
of her? Promise she'll always have the inn? And that you'll
take care of Gabe, too? Jonah isn't bad but he—" she shakes
her head "—can't help but hurt other people. He doesn't
know any better."

"I promise. I do. But you're going to be fine, darling. You'll
be able to take care of them yourself, soon enough."

"Yourself," she repeats, and Lilly senses the slow dawning.
"Myself. Mom. Please, tell me Chase is not dead."

What was Lilly thinking? Why, in that moment, did she
not protect her daughter from the reality that awaited? Now
those exquisite eyes are spilling over with tears that will break
Lilly's heart for the rest of her life. Lilly thinks maybe this is
her do-over, her chance to set it right. But she has no control
over what she says next. "I'm sorry. He's gone," Lilly says.

"No, you're not," Virginia whispers. "You're not sorry at
all. Remember in the summer, those harsh things you said to
him?" Of course Lilly remembers. The way she lost her tem-
per with her son-in-law, the way Virginia responded, with
cold silence at first, and then by taking her inadequate husband and their little family—Gabe included; he was always

included—to that cabin in Quebec, right in the middle of the high season, when Lilly needed her daughter's help the most.

"I *am*," faraway Lilly insists, but from here it feels weak. She can see herself standing at the window of the inn, watching impassively as Chase put the empty beer bottle in the snowbank, walked toward the dock, got in the hovercraft. *Stop him.* But she didn't. She turned away from the window.

Virginia speaks again. "I ran so fast. I asked Jonah for help. I tried. But it was too late." Those blue-green eyes pin Lilly like a butterfly mounted on a spreading board. "Why didn't you believe in him? Why didn't you, why couldn't you, believe in *us*?" So much to say to that, but this is the moment everything stops. Those eyes reflect shock, then pain, then a strange blankness, and Lilly is calling for the nurses, the doctor, George, anyone.

She can hear it, the sound of the flat line, and it's so loud, too loud—Lilly blinks several times. But before she can remember the worst part, the part about how they came in and explained, too late, the type of shock the body could go into during the rewarming process, Virginia is gone.

A nurse has entered Jonah's room. Lilly looks down at all the tubes and wires attached to the man there. Jonah.

Virginia is gone.

A nurse is looking at her. "Excuse me, ma'am? Are you a relative?"

Lilly can't speak.

"Ma'am?"

"If I had been a better mother, he never would have died, and she never would have died either. If I had just been a better mother..."

"It's okay... Now let's just try to calm down," the nurse says. Then she leaves the room and soon there is another nurse who is gently leading her away from the bed and out into the hall.

"Are you family?" this second nurse asks, leading her to a chair.

"She was my daughter."

"You should sit, ma'am. Maybe you're confused? In the wrong room?"

Lilly sits, obedient. She closes her eyes. There's something she's forgetting. Something important. Something she didn't do, turned the kettle off, locked the car door?

Gabe.

She opens her eyes. "Excuse me," she says to a young woman in indigo scrubs. Her face is plain but her hair is re-markable: thick, mahogany, in waves. "Was there a young man here before? Visiting Jonah?"

The nurse's expression reflects sympathy, concern. "Yes," she says. "He was here. His son."

"Do you know if he's coming back?"

"We're trying to reach him now, to tell him his father has died."

Dead. Jonah is dead.

And Lilly has an appointment. That's it. That's what she's here for.

She stands. "I'm late."

"Ma'am, would you like some water, or some tea or any-thing?"

Lilly doesn't answer. She's had enough of the woman's con-descending manner. She's not going to sit in a home for years, drooling onto her collar, staring at a television screen with her hands twisting in her lap. She remembers saying to George, "Please, don't ever let that happen to me." It was after an af-ternoon spent volunteering in the aphasia care center at the hospital, just downstairs. She had been showing one of the patients a picture book of mountain vistas when he became agitated. He kept pointing at the mountains and asking for something, but what? "I'm sorry," Lilly had said. "I'm sorry you can't talk anymore." She had reached for his hand. Eventually, he cried himself to sleep in his chair. She won't be that man. She's going to tell Dr. Turnbull that he needs to put a stop to whatever it is that's happening to her.

"Is there a washroom?"

"Just down that way, on the left. You'll see the sign."

She walks straight past the washroom and escapes the hateful ward. But where was Dr. Turnbull's office? Oh, yes. She wrote it down. She retrieves the piece of paper from the pocket of her cardigan. She finds the intake desk.

"I'm Lilly Summers," she tells the young man behind the reception counter. "I have an appointment."

He shakes his head. "You missed it. We tried to call you at home. You're going to have to reschedule."

"Tell him it's me. We know each other," Lilly says. "I've volunteered here for years."

"I'm sorry, but he's in with another patient now."

He isn't even looking at her; he's staring at his computer screen.

"You're a rude young man," Lilly says before she walks away and makes her way down the stairs and out the doors of the hospital.

There's a record player in the lounge and a bin of records beside it.

Turn it up nice and loud, and you might soon have yourself a little rainy-day party.

My parents prefer Etta James, but I'm into the Beatles.

Gabe gets to the main floor and keeps walking, past the cafeteria doors and toward the main lobby. The double doors at the front of the hospital open and close, open and close. He runs through them, as if they might close a final time and lock him in. A patient stands outside, smoking a cigarette, oblivious to the cold, but Gabe is immediately freezing. He has no coat, no hat, no gloves, no idea what is happening to him. A panic attack? A nervous breakdown?

"Fuck!" He thought he said this inside his head, but a woman passing him clutches her handbag to her chest.

It was soothing, being with Lilly. But with every step he took away from her, out of that hospital room, it all came back. She'd sent him away. And she'd done it because he wasn't good enough to be a part of her family, to be a part of her life. He believed this, because of her. So how could she turn around, all these years later, and casually invite him to dinner? What was he thinking, coming here? The look on her face when he said George had called him! She had no idea. Not a clue. George hadn't even mentioned it to her.

He can't breathe.

He walks until he can no longer feel his hands, until he

has to either breathe or pass out. He gulps air. Then he goes
through the first door he sees. A bar.

When did it happen, exactly, that he fell in love with Mae?
They were kids one minute, and then they weren't and he
was dying for her, following her around like she was drop-
ping crumbs of his soul. He remembers her eighth grade
graduation, when the pangs of longing began. He sat with
Lilly and George near the front of the auditorium. Some of
the girls were gawky, and some of them were almost beautiful, and Mae was just Mae to him, until that night. She still
wore glasses, and her hair was braided around her head, and
as she crossed the stage, Gabe grinned at her and gave her
a thumbs-up, and she grinned back and his heart did something: skipped a beat. He felt like the most special person in
the room, because Mae had grinned at him like that.

That summer, she got contact lenses. One afternoon when
he was working in the boathouse, he saw her out the window, walking down the bank. Her hair was down and she
was wearing a sundress he didn't recognize—white with yellow flowers, gathered around her chest—and for a moment
he didn't recognize her. She was magnificent. She probably
always had been, but he was just noticing. And it wasn't just
her looks: that only sealed the deal in his shallow adolescent
mind. It was everything she was, everything she was becoming. She wasn't like anyone. He loved that about her. She was
thoughtful and kind. She was funny, but mostly only around
him. She didn't try too hard, but she wanted things. He could
tell. And he wanted those things for her. He wanted everything for her. From then on, officially, she wasn't childhood
Mae when she passed him in the halls at school. She was a
young woman and he was falling in love with her. He tried

to conceal these feelings from her for years and he believed he succeeded.

But he couldn't hide it, not from everyone.

One afternoon, he ran into his father in town. He tried to cross the street, but it was too late. "I saw you with her," Jonah said, his voice cruel, disdainful. "Saw you two sitting at Cathy's. Didn't even say hello to your own father." Gabe *had* seen Jonah that day but had steadfastly ignored him until he went away.

"You know there's going to come a time when a girl like that's not gonna want anything to do with a moron like you, right? Because that's what happened with her mother!" Gabe crossed the street then, walked away from his father as fast as he could.

His father never said anything more about Mae, or about Virginia.

It was a late-summer afternoon when Mae and her friend Kate rounded the corner of the inn and walked toward the water, barefoot in their swimsuits, towels around their necks. Gabe was working in the boathouse, cleaning the walls because George had mentioned seeing mold. He had worked at the inn's tiny marina for a few years because, Gabe had explained to George, he wanted to pay off his debt to the Summers family. "You're family," George had answered. "There's no debt." But Gabe had insisted.

Mae was wearing her red two-piece: the fabric was stretching across her chest, revealing a band of firm, golden flesh at her waist, a glimpse of her navel. Gabe had been staring as they approached and Kate said something he didn't hear. He took out his headphones and was embarrassed by the torrent of loud, angry music that rushed forth. He pressed stop on the CD.

"Hell-ooo, McFly, anyone home?" Gabe had never really

liked Kate and wondered sometimes if he was just weirdly jealous of anyone close to Mae.

"Hey, hi," he said. "Going for a swim?"

"Hi, Gabe," Mae called. She ducked her head; he melted. They continued past the dock and toward the bank. But then Mae stopped walking and glanced at Kate and said, "Hang on a sec, I'll meet you down there." Kate shrugged and kept walking toward the water alone.

Mae stepped onto the dock on her tiptoes because she was afraid to get slivers in her feet, Gabe knew. She walked toward him like a dancer. "Got any plans after work?" she asked. It used to be a given that after work they would go for a bike ride or a swim, maybe watch a movie. But this year, that had changed. And not just because he didn't live at the inn anymore. This year, he had started feeling like a guest in her life, like he had to ask permission to spend time with her, and it was adding to the awkwardness growing between them, was encroaching like a weed around everything he'd been feeling that he wished he didn't feel but also knew he couldn't live without.

"Gabe? Are you planning to answer me?"

He tried to sound casual. "Sorry. No plans."

"Want to hang out? Watch movies? I'll rent *The Usual Suspects*... But only if we can watch *Jerry Maguire* again. Or *Legends of the Fall*."

He'd watch *Titanic* a hundred times in a row just to be beside her, but he didn't say so. Instead, he said, "Sure, sounds good."

She looked down at the dock, scuffed a toe back and forth against the wood.

"You'll get a sliver," he warned. She used to cry when she was little and he'd try to pick them out. When she got older she just bit her lip and looked up and blinked, over and over.

He wanted to kiss her feet. Right now. Kneel before her and kiss them.

"Okay, so just…come over later? I'll order pizza. You'll probably be hungry."

"I have to go home. I'll be over by eight." He was living in a rented room in town now, above Garry's Autobody, where he worked part-time. He needed to shower and change; there was no way he was going to sit beside her on the couch all night smelling of motor oil and sweat.

That night, he found her in the den at the back of the inn, the room that was reserved just for family, the room he and Mae had been watching movies and playing board games in forever. There was a pizza box, two cans of Coke and a bag of Sour Cherry Blasters, his favorite. He felt touched and stupid. Why hadn't he thought to bring something for her? "Should I make popcorn?" she asked.

"Nah, it's okay." He opened the box and took a slice— sausage, green olives, pineapple, anchovies; they called it The Weirdo over at the pizza place; it was what he and Mae always ordered—and sat down on the couch beside her.

"You know, I never really see movies with anyone but you." He could feel the heat rise in his face, but it was too late to take his words back.

"Yeah, right. You must take girls to the movies all the time. I never see you anymore."

"That's me. Girls all over the place, raging social life."

She gave him a look he couldn't decode. He grabbed a Coke can, opened it.

"What should we watch first?" she asked.

"Your choice."

"Nah, don't make me pick. Okay, fine, *Usual Suspects*," she said.

"That's not what you *want* to pick. You're just being nice."

She got up and crossed the room to put the tape in, and he could tell from the bounce of her ponytail that she was a little annoyed with him. The movie started and he stared at the screen, eventually lost himself in it a bit; he really did love that film. When he glanced at her later, she was watching him, not the screen.

"Is everything okay with you, Gabe?"

"Yeah. Why?"

"You just seem…different lately."

He couldn't look at her now. She would see everything. His eyes returned to the screen. "Everything's great. Fine."

"Okay. If you say so."

The movie ended. She held up the remote and clicked off the television. "Do you want to go outside, maybe? Lie on the tramp and look at the stars…or something?"

When they were kids, they used to lie on the trampoline—the tramp, they called it—and look at the stars. When did they stop doing that? And why?

"Sounds good," he said.

"I'll get blankets and meet you outside."

He was already lying down when she returned, trying to get his heart rate to slow to a normal pace. "Hey," she said.

He looked up at the sky. It was full of stars, a riot of them. "Look, I'm sorry—you're right, I've been a jerk lately. It's not about you." *It's all about you. Everything is about you.*

"It's okay—I just want to make sure you're fine. I care about you, Gabe. You're like…" But she didn't finish. It didn't matter. He knew what she was going to say. *You're like a brother to me.* He hated this. It used to be enough, but it wasn't anymore.

He fumbled in the long, low pocket of his jeans for his Discman. "Want to listen? It's Wilco."

She put in an earbud and listened for a moment. "Kinda slow and depressing," she said. "It's very you."

This cut him, but he wasn't about to show it. She gave him back his earbud. When she did, she left her arm touching his. He could hear the river, always moving, flowing away from them.

"Look, did you see?" Mae said. "A shooting star."

"Do you know what shooting stars are? Meteors burning up as they hit the earth's atmosphere."

"Of course I know that, Gabe. Everyone knows that."

He was embarrassed. "Sorry. Right. I just—"

But she was laughing. "Think you're smarter than me, I get it. Because you used to help me with my math homework in, what, fifth grade?"

That laugh of hers, that smile of hers. It thawed him. He found himself confessing. "I always feel—" he hesitated "—kind of lucky when I see one. Like, look, hey, another one missed us, the whole world didn't blow up."

"You have the most bizarre sense of humor. *The whole world didn't blow up. Ha.*"

He was smiling now, too. "Admit it, though. It is kind of lucky."

"I know what you mean," she said in a softer voice. "I always feel it, but in a different way. Because the light from the stars is so old—millions of years, right?—so the fact that we can even see that light, the fact that we're still here… You're right. It's lucky."

He watched her lips forming words and imagined the things he always imagined when he looked at those lips. "The time it takes the light from our star to reach us is the distance to the star divided by the speed of its light," he said, because he needed to say something, anything, to rescue himself from this drowning feeling.

Mae angled her body toward him. "You're the smartest person I know," she whispered. "You really should be going to college. Except—"

He watched as shadows fell across the planes on her beautiful, familiar face. She looked at his eyes, then at his mouth. And then—

She kissed him. She pressed her lips against his and when he finally got over his shock enough to respond, he was a new person, a different one altogether. Maybe all of the terrible stories he had told himself over the course of a lifetime weren't true. If Mae was kissing him, maybe he was somehow worthy of it. She paused for a minute. "Mae," he whispered, and she put both hands on his face and pulled him back toward her and their teeth clicked together and they laughed. He held her as if she might break, but eventually he lowered his hands, touched the bare skin of her waist, inched up and cautiously touched the fabric of her bra. Lace on his fingertips. He really couldn't breathe now. If he died in this moment, he would die happy, and he had never imagined that he would die happy.

After a while, she pulled a blanket over them. The curve of her waist, the small of her back, the smooth, soft skin under her bra, the excruciating delight of passing his fingers over one of her nipples and feeling it harden, hearing a tiny moan escape her lips, the sound traveling into his mouth, his only, his alone.

She pulled away. "I can't believe we're doing this."

"You want to, though, right? Or should I—"

"Of course I want to. You do, too— Don't you?"

Everything hinged on what he said next. He could mumble something unintelligible and meaningless, he could say, *The way I feel about you, Mae, is the distance to the stars divided by the speed of their light,* or he could say the right thing. The truth. "I wanted to kiss you more than anything. I've wanted to, Mae, all my life." He looked into her eyes and saw stars reflected back at him. "I love you," he said. It was the biggest risk he'd ever taken.

"I love you, too."

He lost track of time. When their mouths parted, she leaned her head against his chest and he kissed the top of her head. "I love you," he whispered again. And then she fell asleep like that, her head against his heart. He tried not to move too much while she slept. Eventually he slept, too. Even with the light from the stars above them, a dead light, the product of stars that no longer existed, with meteors and asteroids flying around in chaos and nothing anyone could do but breathe a sigh of relief every time life went on, he slept the most peaceful sleep of his life.

A twig snapped and he opened his eyes. George was coming around the corner. "Oh." George stopped.

Mae stirred. Gabe needed to move, and fast. He slid out from under the blanket and swung his legs over the side of the trampoline. There was a look in George's eyes that he had never seen before. It scared him. A meteor, an asteroid slamming into the world: it changes everything. Gabe had let himself forget that.

"I'm really sorry," Gabe said. Why did he say that? It wasn't true. He wasn't sorry, not at all.

But George's expression cleared and he smiled and said, "It's all right. It's only you, Gabe. I was concerned when I didn't see her in her room. She's with you, so I know she's safe. Just make sure she gets into her bed before dawn." He turned then, started to walk away. But he stopped after a few steps and turned back to him. "And, Gabe," he said. "We won't mention this to Lilly."

"Okay," he said. Gabe watched as George disappeared into

the darkness. It unsettled him, George suggesting he say nothing to Lilly. Lilly had never minded before when Gabe was close to Mae, even when he slept in her room. He had been imagining lately that George and Lilly would actually be happy to discover he was in love with their granddaughter.

Gabe climbed back up on the tramp and got underneath the blanket with Mae. Her body was so warm, it felt like coming home to lamp-lit windows and a fire in the hearth. "Everything okay?" she murmured.

"Yes, I was just…stretching my legs."

That's the last moment of happiness he can remember right now.

"Hey, man, you want another one?" The bartender is standing in front of his table, holding the bottle.

"No. Thanks." He pulls money out of his wallet, leaves the half-full glass where it is. He's not drinking bourbon, ever again. He's also not going back to the hospital to face Lilly, to sit beside his father while he wastes away and eventually dies. He doesn't owe that man anything, and being there for him now isn't going to erase his past mistakes, or bring Virginia back, or make him good enough for Mae, or a part of the Summers family. He just isn't, never was.

He should go back to New York City. He should go right now. But he can't. Not yet. He needs to see the cabin one last time, just like he always did. And he needs to be near her—even if the river divides them—just one last time.

Go for a walk. In the rain? Absolutely.
Walking in the rain is the most fun when you stop
worrying about getting wet.

The phone is ringing. Mae opens her eyes, but hesitates. The night before, Lilly said that Peter had called. Could that possibly be true? It keeps ringing. What if it's one of the detectives? What if they've decided she actually is responsible? What if they're going to come for her? She contemplates not answering. It rings again.

They wouldn't call first. They'd bang on the door.

"Hello?"

"May I speak to Lilly Summers, please?"

Mae stands and walks to her bedroom door. "Grandma?" she calls out. Bud woofs in response and comes running. "Grandma?" she calls again. Silence. She must still be at the hospital.

"No, I'm sorry, she's not in at the moment. Can I take a message?"

"Please have her call Dr. Turnbull's office. She's missed her appointment and will need to reschedule." The voice sounds tense and irritable. Mae finds a pen in the drawer of her bedside table and writes down the number.

When she hangs up, Bud is whining, so she goes downstairs and opens the door for him, then stands looking out at the snow-topped cabins and the river in the distance, letting the cold wind blow in and through the house, though she knows her grandparents wouldn't approve.

A man is walking down the riverbank. She thinks she imagines him, at first, another one of these spectral men, these Gabe-but-not-Gabes she's conjured up.

But this one exists. She blinks and blinks again, and he's still there. And Bud's ears have perked up and he's growling in that direction. He's tall, with dark hair. He's not wearing a coat, and it's twenty below. Is it the same man she saw earlier, now coming back from wherever he went?

"Bud!" she calls, and he comes running back toward the door. She steps inside and gets her coat, shoves a tuque over her hair, finds Bud's leash and snaps it on. Then she starts down the road.

The Gabe she knew always returned to that island when his father called him back. And now Jonah is sick—so could it be...?

She starts walking toward the river.

But when she gets to the edge, she can't. She stares down at the footprints and breathes in frightened gasps as she tries not to envision her parents slipping under, slipping away.

But another memory is waiting when that one is defeated. And it won't leave her alone. As she watches the man climb the bank of Island 51, she remembers the night she found out Gabe was not who she thought he was.

Mae stood at the window in the lobby, waiting. For him. She was wearing a blue dress. Her hair was freshly washed and conditioned; her heart was pounding. Gabe had said he had a surprise but she already knew: his motorcycle, the one he'd been working on since before their first kiss, all summer and fall at Garry's.

As soon as she saw Gabe riding up the driveway, her own

personal James Dean, she knew she was going to get on the back of that bike—even though her grandmother had heard about the bike in town and demanded she never ride on it. Lilly and George were away, visiting friends across the border in Kingston. They wouldn't be home until morning.

She slid on her sandals and ran out the front door. She threw her arms around Gabe's neck and kissed him. She loved the surprised look he always had after they kissed: like someone had just given him an unexpected gift. Kissing Gabe was a revelation for her, too, every single time.

"It's kind of sexy, you know—the idea of you as a mechanic, covered in oil."

"I don't know about sexy. I think I even have motor oil in my teeth. Tell me if you taste any."

She laughed.

"Here, I have a helmet for you." He opened the seat and took out a black helmet, smaller than his, and new. She liked the idea that he went out and got it for her, that he was thinking of her when they weren't together. Because she was always thinking about him. Writing poems she never showed him, doodling hearts everywhere with their initials, trying out different combinations of their names. *Mae Summers-Broadbent. Mae Broadbent. Mae and Gabriel Broadbent.*

She put on the helmet and climbed behind him, wrapping her arms around his waist. She imagined taking his shirt off, feeling his skin against hers. He backed slowly down the driveway. They rode alongside the river and away from town. She made a dozen wishes on the wind, two dozen, three, too many to count. She squeezed her arms around him, shouted through her helmet, "Can you pull over for a minute?"

He slowed down then pulled onto the shoulder, removed his helmet and looked at her. "Are you all right?"

She took off her helmet. "I'm great," she said. "My grand-

parents aren't coming home tonight." He didn't say anything.
Had she miscalculated, made a mistake? But then he put his
helmet back on and she did the same. Within moments, they
were back in the driveway of the inn. He turned off the bike.
She took off her helmet again. She could hear crickets, the
flow of river water, the tick of the cooling engine. "I love
you," she said.

"I love you, too, Mae. I always have." She made a vow to
herself in that moment: *This is not my first love: it will be my
only love.* A curse, in the end.

Once they got to her bedroom, she felt self-conscious.
There should be candles, music—she should have planned
this, right? She did have a condom, hidden in her end table
drawer; she got it from Kate, who had been having sex with
her longtime boyfriend, Mark. Kate had frowned when Mae
had asked for it. "You should also go on the pill, you know.
And, Mae, are you sure? You two have been together for only
a few weeks. And Gabe is just so…"

So…what? Why was everyone so against Gabe all of a sudden? "He's been my best friend my entire life."

"Hey! I thought I was your best friend!"

Her cheeks felt hot, and there was a sudden warmth in the
base of her belly. She took the condom out of the drawer, and
Gabe's eyes widened. "Mae, are you sure?"

"Positive. Absolutely. I've never been so sure about anything in my life." Not true. She was unsure and terrified, but
soon it didn't matter because they were kissing again and then
they were taking off their clothes—there was no way to do
this gracefully; Mae was quickly learning that real life was
nothing like the sex scenes in movies. She pressed her mouth
against his shoulder to keep from crying out: the combination of pleasure and pain was startling and new.

He pulled back and looked into her eyes. "Are you okay? I

don't want to hurt you," he said in a new voice, a voice of his she had never heard, a voice struggling for control. It made her feel powerful, beautiful, perfect.

"You're not. Not hurting me. Please, don't stop."

Then, "Always," she said to him. "Always, always, always."

"Always," he said back. He pressed his face into her shoulder and she felt his body shake, for just a moment, and she put her arms around him and held him against her. She was sure that they were the only two people in the world who had ever loved like this, that maybe even, in that moment, they were the only two people in the world at all.

Except they weren't.

Mae heard the front door of the inn open and the voices of her grandparents. "I thought you said they weren't coming home," Gabe whispered.

"They weren't." They dressed quickly. Just in time. There was a knock on the bedroom door.

"Mae? Are you in there?"

"Yes, Grandma. I just need a minute."

"Can we speak to you? *Both* of you? In the kitchen?"

They came downstairs wordlessly and sat beside each other; she held his hand. George was sitting beside Lilly, staring intently at the surface of the harvest table. Lilly's face was white with anger. But why?

"I'd like you to leave," Lilly said. "I'd like you to leave this house, right now."

Mae gasped, turned to her grandfather, but he wouldn't look up. Gabe was standing and backing from the room. She stood, too, but Lilly said, "Mae! *You* stay here."

She didn't want to, but she did. She wondered later what would have happened if she'd gone after Gabe.

Lilly turned to her now, her voice cold and harsh. "Mae, Gabe's not for you."

"What are you talking about? Gabe is a part of our family!"

"This has gone too far. I should have stopped it earlier."

Mae implored her grandfather. "Are you going to just sit there? This is insane."

George cleared his throat. He looked up from the table finally. "Your grandmother is doing what she thinks is best," he said.

Mae banged both palms against the table. "Did it ever occur to either of you that it wasn't him, that it was me, that this is what *I* wanted?" George looked away again. Lilly's mouth was a hard slit and Mae didn't recognize her. In the silence that followed, she was almost sure she could hear Gabe's motorcycle in the distance, getting farther and farther away. She pushed her chair away from the table.

"I'm going after him," she said. "I'm going into town."

"You will do no such thing," Lilly said. "You will stay in this house if you still want to live in it."

Mae's mouth dropped open. Gabe was all she had, but so were her grandparents. She turned and went to the stairs, climbed them slowly, felt the tears begin to slide down her cheeks. Once she was in her room, she made a plan in her head. She would call Gabe in a few minutes, whisper into the phone, arrange to meet him the next day, tell him everything was going to be fine. She'd let Lilly cool down. In the morning, everything would be different. Lilly would apologize. Gabe would come over. Life would go on. Normal.

When she called, he didn't answer the phone.

She was right, though, but only about one thing: in the morning, everything *was* different.

Lilly was waiting for her in the kitchen. Her grandfather was standing by the window, staring out at the boathouse.

"Gabe stole from us," Lilly announced when Mae walked in, bleary-eyed and heart sore from the night before, from hearing the phone ring and ring, from wondering why Gabe wouldn't talk to her.

"What are you talking about?"

George turned from the window, his voice sad, empty—the voice of a man who was losing someone, someone he had considered a son. "The boathouse safe was open, empty, when I went down this morning," he said.

Mae felt her knees weaken. She gripped the table to keep herself standing.

Lilly spoke. "I don't know if he did it while he was here, or if he came back last night."

"Why are you assuming it was him? It could have been anyone!"

"No, Mae," George said.

"How can you be so sure?"

"Because," Lilly said. "I went into town to talk to him, and he was gone. Garry said he'd taken off on his bike and wasn't coming back. Gave him the rent for next month in cash, and rode away with a hockey bag on his back."

Mae sank to the floor. "No. I don't believe it."

"I'm sorry," Lilly said, and it sounded like she was apologizing for something.

Eventually, Mae got up off the floor. She went upstairs. She waited for a call from Gabe, for some kind of explanation. But he didn't call. She went into town later to see for herself that he was gone. He was. She went back to the inn and she waited. Days, weeks.

She didn't get the note until a month later. George was taking the trampoline down for the winter. It was something Gabe would normally have done. George knocked on her bedroom door.

"Come in."

"I found it rolled up in a spring. I think it was meant for

you." He handed her the note. He patted her arm and looked at her for a long moment. It hurt him, too, what Gabe had done. She unrolled the paper and read two lines: *I will always love you. And I'm sorry. Gabe.*

She walked down to the river and threw the note in the water.

Her eyes have become unfocused from staring so long at the river, at the footprints. That note, long ago swallowed by the river, might still be out there in some form, under the ice. And Gabe, he might be out there, too, in his father's cabin.

She slides down the snow and ice-covered riverbank until she's standing on the river before the path of footprints.

Go on an island cruise in the rain.

There are way more than 1,000 islands.

I think that's just where they lost count.

Gabe sits at the kitchen table. He sits on the couch. He paces the hall. Finally, he stops and places his hand on the door of the room he's been avoiding. He holds his hand there, as if trying to feel what's inside. Then he opens the door.

Nothing has changed. The *Dukes of Hazzard* poster on the wall, now so sun bleached the images have turned to blue-green shadows; the army-issue sleeping bag on the cot; the *Star Wars* pillowcase Mae gave him for Christmas one year.

He walks over to the dresser: there's a pile of change on top, a Hardy Boys book, a blank tape that says MIX on it in Mae's handwriting. And nothing is dusty. This gives him pause. His father was dusting, in here? It seems impossible, but— He picks up the Hardy Boys book and sits down on the cot with it. His father is in the hospital, dying in a hospital bed. He should be there, shouldn't he? It's his duty, isn't it? But that man… The words on the page blur. He feels small, like a boy. An eight-year-old boy.

"You little shit, this is all your fault!" Gabe's nose was bleeding. He covered his head, tried to shield his face, as his father started hitting him again.

"I told you. I told you exactly what you needed to do! I even wrote it down for you. You had one goddamn job to do before we sold that hovercraft to Virginia—and you didn't do it, did you? *Did you?*"

Gabe remembers. All he had wanted to do was get across the river to play with Mae. So he'd ignored his father's instructions, but later, had told him the job was done. "No. I'm sorry, I'm sorry, I'm *sorry!*"

"It's not me you should be saying sorry to. It's your little friend Mae. You killed her parents. You realize that, don't you? Because of you, her parents are dead." Every slow word burned into Gabe's brain.

He killed them. He killed her parents. "Please... I didn't mean to!"

"You're lucky I don't go to the police."

Could he go to jail for this? Could kids be sent to prison? There would be so many bad people there. And he wouldn't see Mae ever again. He started to rock. *No, no, no.*

"You're lucky I don't kill you," Jonah said.

"Go ahead, just do it!" Gabe shouted before he could stop himself. Then he put his hands over the wet spot on his pants. Blood dripped from his nose onto his sleeping bag.

Jonah backed out of the room.

Gabe heard the boat start. He stayed on his bed. Maybe he slept. Later, when he heard the front door open again, he thought his father was back to kill him.

"Gabe?"

Not his father. George.

Gabe pushed himself to a seated position. His pants were still wet and his legs itched and he knew he smelled bad.

"Gabe?"

Gabe was shocked by what happened next: George, a

grown man, began to weep. "We're going to get you out of here for good. I'm so sorry. We should have done this before."

Before he killed Virginia and Chase.

Gabe got off his bed and crossed the room to stand in front George. He wasn't sure what to do with this crying man, so he offered his hand. George reached out and took it, shook it gently, as if they were meeting for the first time. "You're a very good boy, Gabe. You're a good, *good* boy."

Not true. He was bad. He was so, so bad.

"Let's go. Pack what you need and come with me. You're okay now. You're going to come live with us, son."

Son.

That was the moment he should have told George, should have said he was the killer of Mae's parents. He should have said that he was the worst boy ever and volunteered to go to jail because he was so bad.

But Gabe said nothing.

George waited while Gabe packed a bag. He took his hand and led him from the cabin. Gabe got in George's boat. And he went to the inn, and he let these people take care of him when they knew nothing about his horrible secret.

Gabe collapses back on the cot and closes his eyes. Oblivion comes quickly. He thinks he hears a banging at the door, but who would be out here?

When he hears her voice he's sure he must be dreaming.

Do something, anything, you've never done before.

M ae steps into the first icy footprint. Bud bounds toward her. He has a small branch in his mouth, which he presents to her. She throws it and he chases it, brings it back. She throws it farther and off he goes.

To further calm herself, she tries to pretend she's walking on a road, but it's impossible to convince herself that the river is not the river, so she thinks, *I'm walking on several feet of ice, and the ice is not going to break and I'm not going to die out here and I have to see if Gabe is out there because if it's him, I need to ask him why.* She takes another step. Another. Soon she's made it, up the bank and over. The river hasn't claimed her. She's safe.

She approaches the shack and knocks. Silence. She tries the knob. It's not locked. She pushes the door open. "Hello?"

Mae has never been inside this cabin; she wanted to, begged Gabe to take her there on his boat every spring and summer, whenever Jonah wasn't home, but he would never do it. "Think of the worst place you can imagine, and multiply it by ten," he said to her once. She had imagined someplace exactly like this, with its particleboard walls, cracked linoleum on the kitchen floor, dusty surfaces, grimy windows, some of them broken and boarded over, and the smell: dank, neglected, rotten. She trails snow behind her as she passes through the small rooms.

Down the narrow hall, she can hear snoring.

She finds him on a cot, curled up, his head on a stained pillow. Gabe's hair is darker than it used to be and past his collar, thick. His face is covered in stubble. He's older now, his face more defined and set, but he's who he always was, who he was going to be when she knew him, at least as far as looks go.

She steps closer. He's wearing a soft-looking navy hoodie and salt-stained Blundstones, and there's a Hardy Boys book beside him, broken spined and splayed. She turns a slow circle. This was his room when he was a kid. And there's something strange about it. Unlike the rest of the cabin, it's clean in here. No dust. You can see out the window.

She leans in and it hits her: the smell of alcohol on his breath and skin. Her stomach twists upon itself and she's out the door of the bedroom before she fully comprehends what she's doing. She searches for kindling, relights the dying embers in the woodstove, heads to the kitchen to pour water into a chipped mug. It's only when she's standing at the threshold of his room again that she sees what she's done, feels the muscle memory in her actions. She took care of her father, too, when he smelled that way. She could never stop herself. She's about to turn back, to dump the water on the fire and put the mug back, but her footfall causes the wood beneath the linoleum to squeak. Gabe opens his eyes.

"What the...?" he says. He squints. "Mae?"

"Hi." Her voice is curt. Her heart bangs against her rib cage.

"What are you doing here? *How* are you here?"

"I walked. Here, take this." She steps forward, but he doesn't take the mug. He chuckles, and it's that dry, familiar chuckle and it hits her directly in her racing heart, like he's lobbed something at her and she's caught it with her chest.

"But you would never walk across the frozen river. I'm dreaming, right?"

"Not a dream." She shoves the mug into his hands. "Just drink it. Please."

"Thanks." While he drinks, she stands over him, motherly, then backs away. A safer distance.

He moves to the edge of the bed and stands. He's taller now. There are faint lines around his eyes and the silhouette of a beard on his cheeks. He's staring right into her, the way he always could. Her heart has recovered from the earlier blow and it rushes toward him as if no time has passed. She pulls back on it, hard. *No.*

"I saw you," she says. "I thought it was your dad, but then Lilly told me he's sick, and I realized it might be you and I came out here. It was stupid. I shouldn't have."

"Why was it stupid?"

When she doesn't answer, he continues to stare at her as if still trying to determine whether she's real.

"Are you drunk?" she asks.

He runs a hand back and forth over his stubble and looks up at the ceiling. "Not really. I saw Lilly at the hospital. She said I should come to the inn for dinner. Instead, I went to a bar."

She feels it now: a flash fire as the shock wears off. Anger, first in her fingertips, then up her arms. "You...seriously? You saw her, got drunk and now you want to come for dinner like nothing ever happened?"

He's looking at a salt stain on one of his boots. "I don't want to come to dinner. That's why I left."

"You stole from us. Then you disappeared. And *you* don't want to come for dinner?" Her laugh is bitter. "This is ridiculous."

"Stole," he repeats, and his eyes are back on her. There's anguish there now. "You're right. I'm sorry. I took so much from you—"

"I don't want an apology! I don't care if you're sorry! That's not why I'm here. I want you to explain. Why would you steal money and leave, why would you do that to me, to us? After everything we did for you. After everything we—" She presses her palms against her cheeks and her fingers over her eyes to stop the tears. When she's sure she's okay again, she takes her hands away. "They would have given you the money, I'm sure, if you'd just asked. You were like family. And that's why I can't understand why you—"

"I didn't steal any money."

"Don't lie. You never used to lie."

"Lilly gave me money and told me to go. I didn't steal anything."

She narrows her eyes and looks into his. Incomprehension is all she sees. It scares her. "Stop this. The night you left, you went to the boathouse and you stole all the money from the safe. And then you took off."

"I have no idea what you're talking about."

"Fuck you."

"Mae—"

"You used me. You used *my family*. For years. You pretended you were someone you weren't, my best friend, my *everything*—"

He's touching her now, his hands are on her arms and she rears back, but the room is too small for her to get far enough away from him.

"Who told you this?" he asks her.

"My grandmother."

The confusion on his face is replaced by slow realization. And hurt. "I see," he says.

"She wouldn't lie to me."

"Right."

"This is who you've become? You're accusing my grand-mother of lying?"

"All I said was 'right.'"

"I know that sarcastic tone of yours. I know you." As she says this, she realizes it isn't true, she doesn't know this person, standing before her, lying. She never did. "Do you know something? I hate you. You disgust me."

He flinches, but says nothing. She squeezes past him, tries not to touch him but doesn't succeed; their arms brush. *Gabe, Gabe, Gabe,* and then she's in the hall again, thank God. She hasn't taken off her coat or boots so there's nothing for her to do but head through the kitchen and out.

"Bud!" she calls, and he gallops around the side of the cabin. "Come." *Slam.* She starts to run, forgetting her fear of the ice and focusing instead on her fear of the truth.

There's an animal shelter in town with dogs and cats

that need love.

Ask if you can play with them.

You'll feel so good—and so will they.

"Here! Turn left. Summers' Inn. This is where I live."

Lilly collapses against the seat and is able to breathe again. It was difficult to ignore the concerned glances the taxi driver directed at her in the rearview mirror on the trip home from the hospital, and nearly impossible to ignore the panic in her heart, but she managed. "Just drive to Alexandria Bay," she kept telling the driver. "When we get there, I'll know."

The taxi driver turns the car into the driveway. She sees the weather vane on the snowy roof, a beacon to home and safety, and the only place she knows. She can't leave, not now. Why has it been so difficult to make George understand this?

"Thirty-six dollars," the driver says.

"Heavens." George wouldn't approve, but George isn't here. George is gone. He took the car. Didn't he? Or did she leave the car at the hospital? She hates this feeling, the black pit of not knowing and the embarrassment of having to ask people to answer the simplest questions.

The driver comes around to open the door and help her out. She stands in front of the inn and watches him pull away, waves like he's an old friend. Then she hears barking and sees Mae walking up the driveway. "You're home!" she calls out. It occurs to Lilly that perhaps Mae also got lost; she has a peculiar look on her face. *What is she doing here, anyway? Wasn't she supposed to be in New York City?*

"Is everything all right, dear?" Now that she's closer, Lilly can see that Mae's eyes are red and she's been crying, or still is crying.

Mae has dropped the dog's leash. "I need you to tell me the truth about Gabe," she says.

"Oh! I saw him today, too," Lilly says. "And then I lost him. And then he ran away." She's in the black pit now, and she hates that this is happening in front of Mae. But Mae doesn't seem to notice.

"Tell me about what really happened with him the night he left."

The dog—*what is his name?* He eats snow and sneezes, the daft creature. She wishes Mae hadn't come home in this instant. She needs only a few minutes to gather up her thoughts again. These interludes are becoming more frequent, but they never last for long.

"It's so nice to have a dog around," Lilly says.

"Grandma."

"Yes?"

"Would you please look at me? Would you please stop pretending you don't know what I'm talking about?"

Lilly hears the words but doesn't know what they mean. She can only wait and hope for a clue.

"I walked out to Island 51. And I confronted Gabe about stealing from us. Do you know what he said?"

The smile is fading from Lilly's lips. "No, I don't know." A shadow, though. There's a shadow of a memory tugging at her sleeve. Gabe said something to her once, about a burden he was carrying. She should have taken it from him—but she didn't. She tries to chase that memory, but it eludes her.

"He said it didn't happen. He said he didn't steal from us.

He said you gave him the money. And I don't want to believe him, I want to think it's something you never would
have done—but I can't. I have to hear it straight from you.
The truth."

"The money?"

Mae clenches her jaw. "Did he steal it, or did you give it
to him?"

The seconds flow past.

It's so cold. Lilly stamps her feet to keep the feeling in them.
The money, the money. And something about Gabe.

"Gabe didn't steal the money," she says, finally, and she's
rewarded—or punished, she's not sure, she's so unsure—by
a memory as clear and cutting as the night air biting at her
cheeks. Gabe's face. An eighteen-year-old boy in tears is a
difficult thing to witness. She closes her eyes for a moment
and when she opens them again she doesn't see falling snow
anymore. She sees Gabe as he was.

That long ago night, after the shouting and the crying,
after Lilly had banished Gabe from her home, she'd waited
until everyone was in bed, then driven into town. There had
been an envelope, thick with cash, hidden in the depths of
her purse. Had she planned it? Not exactly. But as soon as the
idea came to her, she realized this had always been something
she was going to have to do.

Gabe's apartment had surprised her: tidy, comfortable,
books on a shelf, a desk stocked with drawing pencils, sheets
of white paper, a photograph of Mae tacked to the wall, an
image Lilly didn't recognize, a look of devotion in Mae's eyes
that was unsettling.

They sat at his tiny kitchen table, and she slid her hand
into her purse and clutched the envelope.

"You have to go. You have to take this opportunity I'm
about to give you and leave here, start a new life."

He had ignored her words. "How is Mae? Is she okay?"

"It will be less painful this way. Next year, she'll go to New York for school anyway, and what are you going to do, follow her there, be her lapdog?"

"Well, I was thinking, I mean, maybe. I've always wanted to go to—"

"She won't respect you for clinging to her, and it will ruin your relationship. You'll have nothing left in the end, not even your friendship." He was silent, so she continued. "We care about what happens to you, so we don't want you to leave with nothing. We want to help you. Leaving is what's best for you, and for her. Before it's too late."

Gabe shook his head when she tried to put the envelope in his hand.

"It's a lot of money," Lilly said.

"You don't understand. I love her."

"You're young."

"It's not— I always have. And the other thing…" His voice was breaking, those tears were coming back. "The thing is, I have to take care of her. Not just because I love her, so much, but because I promised. And I owe her, after—"

"You don't owe her anything. And you really can't stay tied to her, tied to this town."

"But—"

"You don't want to end up like your father, do you? Living in a shack? Turning to drink?" It was a knife twist and he drew back from it.

"No," he said, his voice a wound. "No, I don't want to end up like my father. But please, just listen to me. There's something you need to know." What he told her next, it was so absurd. How could a father let a son believe something like that? Lilly supposed she shouldn't have been surprised. With Jonah Broadbent, any level of cruelty was possible—

but still, she was surprised. She looked at the boy she had taken in as her own and knew that if she told the truth, she would heal him.

But she couldn't. It was him or Mae. And she had always known she would choose her granddaughter.

"You can never make this up to her. Don't you see? Your relationship is even more doomed than I thought it was."

A gasp. A female voice. "Why would you do that to him?"

Lilly's eyes refocus. She had been speaking out loud, and she hadn't realized. Mae is in front of her, her cheeks wet with tears or snow or both. Words are lost, then found, in the falling snow. What Lilly has said, it's the wrong thing yet again. But maybe she can make it right.

"I lost your mother to a man with a drinking problem, a man with a bad childhood he never recovered from. I wasn't about to lose you to that, too."

"How could you make that assumption? He was eighteen! How did you know who he was going to become? We needed each other! And you didn't even give us a chance!"

"I lost a child," she says. "No one understands what happens to you, when you lose a child. You do things, you feel things." Lilly's head aches. She desperately wants the comfort of petting the dog. Where is he? She wants to call for him but she can't, because you can't call for an animal when you don't know his name.

"Why won't you look at me? Answer me! Tell me how you could have done this!"

"I'm trying!" In Lilly's ears, her voice sounds like that of a frightened child. "I did it for you," she says, attempting to sound more in control.

"No. Don't say that."

"I thought he was going to ruin your life."

"So you ruined his?"

Enough. Enough of this. "I'm very tired. I'm very cold. I need to go inside. We can discuss this later." Lilly keeps her voice firm. She is the adult, Mae is the child. Not the other way around. *Why don't children have respect anymore?*

"I'm not sure I can talk to you about this ever again," Mae says in a voice colder than the night Lilly is being forced to stand in.

"Please…" Lilly sees she will always be out in the cold now. This was not a secret that should ever have been revealed. It's too much. Her head, her heart, too much pain. She just needs to lie down. If she could just rest she's sure it will become clear, the path toward getting Mae to forgive her for this, and maybe even to getting George to forgive her. To getting them both to forgive her for the things she did for them because she loved them.

"What you did was wrong," Mae says. "And I have to find a way to make it right." She turns away from Lilly and heads down the driveway, back the way she came. As Lilly watches her, Mae begins to run. *You can't chase her. She's just like Virginia. Wherever she's going, you can't stop her.*

The dog is nosing at Lilly's hip, so she picks up his lead. Inside, where it's warm. That's where she needs to go. But instead, she starts to walk. She follows Mae, because she never chased Virginia, and Virginia is dead.

But when she gets to the end of the driveway, there is no Mae. An empty street and snow falling thick. Did she ever exist, her granddaughter? *Of course she did.* Lilly turns left, then right, then stops walking and looks up at the sky. "Where do I go?" she asks. No answer. She holds her bare hands in front of her eyes and chooses left, then disappears into the falling snow, the dog leading the way.

If it's raining, one of us will have lit a fire.

Pull up a chair, find a book—and enjoy.

The cabin door slams. Gabe stands, frozen, in the doorway of his childhood bedroom. Then he runs down the hall to the living room window. She's already sliding down the bank and onto the river.

She was here. And I let her go.

He sits on the couch. It stinks like his old man. Of course Lilly told Mae he stole. It all makes sense. She loved him as a child, but hated him as his love for Mae grew and changed—and became something that was less than what Mae deserved.

And it was bad enough that he thought he was good enough for Mae—but when he told Lilly his horrible secret about Mae's parents the night she came to see him, she sent him away. And she was right to do it.

He stands and walks to the window. Mae's walking fast, almost halfway across the river with the dog running ahead. The sun is low in the sky. He got to see her one last time. He'd always wondered what she was like as an adult, and now he knows: different, but also the same. An orange tuque over her long curls, that color, kind of blond, kind of brown, with a little red. He's never seen it on anyone else. The prettiest color in the world. Her voice: a little huskier than it used to be. Sexy, and appealing. Her eyes: a sadness there, a sadness he didn't like to see. He had always believed that staying away, per Lilly's instructions, would guarantee Mae's happiness. Her eyes were angry, too. She was mad as hell at him and those sad eyes were flashing with it. She pushed him away and she ran. Smart woman.

He turns away from the window and takes one last look around the cabin. The night he left, he crossed the river on a borrowed boat to get a few things. Or maybe he wanted to say goodbye to his father, because he was that stupid. Jonah had been sober that night, or almost. Not drunk *yet*. He took one look at Gabe, packing books and tapes into a bag, and said, "Ah. It finally happened. They sent you on your way."

Gabe said nothing, just kept packing. "Don't take it too hard, boy. No one was good enough for Virginia, and no one will be good enough for Mae either. Not you, that's for sure. You're better off moving on."

"Don't come back," he said when Gabe was at the door, but he didn't say it in a cruel way. What was it in Jonah's voice that night that made it different than usual? Sadness, relief. He had been a father commiserating with a son on the harshness of the world, a father letting a son go.

Gabe hadn't listened to him. He'd decided to return when he should have stayed away, when, for once, Jonah had been right. He thinks about Jonah, alone in that hospital room. He'll die alone, or maybe he's already dead. That doesn't matter. Jonah would want him to leave, to finally do the right thing.

He'll go into town now, he'll find out when the next train is, and he won't look back when he goes this time. Alexandria Bay will cease to exist, and so will Mae.

He took something away from her, she's right. He had started to apologize, but her anger had made him realize that in this case the truth was going to be worse. Mae wasn't for him, and there was never going to be anything he could do to change that fact.

Read a dime-store romance.

Don't be embarrassed: people need love stories.

When Mae got back to the cabin, he was gone. He had poured water on the embers of the fire. There was nothing left of him except a slight divot in the bed where he had been lying. "Gabe!" she called. But she was calling to a ghost.

Back on shore now, she stands with her hands on her knees, gasping. The gloaming has descended, transitioning day into night. She made it ashore just in time. The snow falls hard now, the kind of thick flakes that cause the world to go quiet. Did he have a car, or did he take the bus here? And where is he going, where does he even live? She doesn't know—but she knows he's running away and that she has to stop him from getting too far or she'll never see him again, for real this time.

She strides down Market Street, cutting a path that is erased by the snow as she goes, and pauses in front of The Ship. Inside, she approaches the little reception desk. "Did a man just check in, Gabriel Broadbent?"

The clerk is wearing dirty eyeglasses. He looks like he's in his forties, but his cheeks are covered in pimples. "I can't give out information about our guests."

"Oh, come on."

The clerk's shoulders slump. "No one has checked in today at all."

"You're sure?"

"It's February in Alex Bay. Pretty sure, Mae."

"How do you know my name?"

"We went to high school together. You were in my AP chemistry class."

"Oh." She looks more closely, but she doesn't recognize him. "Is my grandfather staying here? George Summers? Please, just tell me."

The clerk adjusts his glasses, then says, "The old guy? Yep, still staying here."

Mae considers. "Can you give him a message for me, please? Can you tell him I'm home and that he needs to come home, too, right away, no matter what?"

"Will do." Somehow she doubts it. She's probably not the first woman to come in here begging.

Back out on the street a car passes slowly and she looks in the window. But it's not Gabe.

She turns down Church Street and stops in front of the Riverboat bar. The door opens and Mae's heart seizes. But it's two middle-aged men fumbling for cigarette packs, exclaiming over the blizzard, folding their bodies around lighters. She looks inside, still feeling hope. She imagines him on a bar stool, head bent over a novel. But he's not there.

She walks in a square through the blizzard-blanketed town. He's not at Skiffs, not at the Sunken Rock, not hunched over a mug at Coffee Pot Cathy's the way his father used to be. Signs on doorways list winter hours for the other establishments. Most windows are dark. Soon, there's nowhere else to look. "Gabe," she says into the night. "Where have you gone?"

There's a car approaching, and at first she thinks she's seeing it wrong, the light on the top that says Taxi. She lifts her arm half-heartedly—if you want a taxi in Alex Bay in winter, you have to call in advance.

"Hop in," says the driver, an older man wearing a black cap. "Where to?"

"Watertown. The bus depot."

"You sure about this? It'll take a while in this weather. I know because I just drove a fellow out there."

Mae clutches the back of the seat in front of her. "Was he… Did he…"

"Younger guy. Dark hair. Big backpack," he offers with a sympathetic smile.

"Was there a bus when you got there?"

"No bus, not yet."

"Take me there. Please."

Headlights illuminate the bus depot, a squat cinderblock building, half-shingled, in the middle of a parking lot. They had tailed it for about a block, and now the bus is pulling in ahead of them. "Could you wait?" she asks the taxi driver, already breathless. "Do you mind?"

She runs toward the building, singularly focused on the bus's lights turning the snow into hundreds of wintry moths. She hears the rumble of the engine, the thudding of her feet, her heart. Around the back of the bus, she starts to slide on ice, almost falls, feels empty space and no one to catch her—but then there he is, stepping up and onto the bus. Dark hair and a backpack. "Gabe!"

He stops moving but doesn't turn around. She runs until she's in front of the open bus doors. Snow falls and melts down her cheeks. She wills him to look at her.

There is the sharp, clean smell of winter all around, combined with oil and exhaust. It reminds her of when they were young, of being with him after he'd been working at the garage or on boats at the marina. Whenever she has inhaled these scents since, she's thought of him.

"Don't go," she says. And finally, he turns. The bus is gearing up already, she can hear it.

A voice reaches her. It's not his. "You need to step inside so I can close the doors."

"Don't go," she says again as her hand lands in his. Warm skin, *his* skin.

Gabe doesn't move.

"Come on, buddy. On or off?"

"I believe you," she says. "That you didn't know what I was talking about. I know you didn't take the money. I'm sorry."

Gabe glances behind him, addresses the driver. "Can I have a minute?"

"Ten seconds. Not a second more."

Gabe steps down, ducks his head toward her and speaks in a low, urgent voice. "Listen, don't apologize to me. You don't have to, you shouldn't, ever. I'm the one who's sorry, and it's too late to say why, too late to say anything. And I have to go. Right now." He's backing away.

"It *isn't* too late. Don't get on that bus, Gabe."

He shakes his head. She's not getting through. Gabe was good at building things, always, especially walls. She used to know how to get beyond them. It used to be so easy.

An impulse: she pulls up the sleeve of his sweatshirt, and the faint circular scar is still there on his forearm. She rubs her thumb across it, touches him the way she used to when she believed he would always be hers.

"Stay with me, Gabe. This time, stay. Please." The snow swirls between them again and she loses sight of his face. But she has hold of him.

"I know everything. Lilly told me all of it, and it's awful, that you ever believed what happened with my parents was your fault. You were a little boy. You were just a kid. You didn't do it on purpose." She feels him shake, like he's about to pull away from her, but he doesn't. "No one should ever have hurt you like that, not your father, not my grandmother and not me by not believing in you. I'm so, so sorry. Please don't leave."

"Last chance," calls the driver. Mae keeps her hand where it is. She's afraid to move. And then she hears it, a voice in her head. *Sometimes when you're afraid, you just have to do the thing that scares you most.*

Mae does the only thing she can think to do, the only thing left: she pulls until he's as close to her as she can get him. She stands on her toes, she finds his mouth through the snow and the cold, the confusion and the regret.

He was always there, waiting for her. And it's easy, once you remember where you are. It's like finding your way home.

His backpack drops from his shoulders and both his arms are around her, on her back, in her hair, touching her cheeks, pulling her closer, closer. He tastes like mint, he tastes the way the snow smells, he tastes just the way she remembers and he feels the same way, too, like the most familiar place in the world, even after all this time.

When they resurface, the bus is long gone, but she says it again, just to be sure. "Don't go."

"I won't," he says in a voice as familiar as her own. "Never again. I promise."

The snow has nestled around them. They know it can't be true, but they both believe it then: that it's just the two of them, that nothing can ever hurt them again. That they are the only two people on earth.

Do a crossword puzzle.

Not only are they fun, they're good for your brain.

L illy walks slowly. There's ice, even at the side of the road. Where did Mae go, and why? *I am taking the dog for a walk. The dog must be walked.* There's such purpose in having a dog. She wishes they'd gotten one before.

She realizes she's on her regular path, the one she normally walks after dinner with Viv. She should have stopped at Viv's house, knocked on her door. Then she wouldn't be alone. But she forgot all about Viv. It's happening again. The spells are becoming more frequent. Soon, they will be all she is. She doesn't want that.

Lilly steps down and goes farther along the river than she intended to. She can't help herself. She wants to look out at the vast, cold expanse, to listen for the cracks and booms, to hear the great sounds that give her such pleasure and never startle her the way they startle others. "Good boy," she says to the dog, because he has stopped pulling and is walking beside her. He wags his tail.

Mae. Where did she go?

She was angry.

Lilly has a wild impulse to step onto the river ice, to clear off a patch by shuffling the snow with her boots, to slide and slip, to feel momentum again. Of course, that would be foolish. But she does it anyway. Then she stands, mischievous, the ice below her feet.

Where am I?

On the river.

She needs to find the riverbank. She needs to find Mae. She needs to go back the way she came—but which way is that? There. She sees a house ahead and feels hopeful. It's not home, though: no weather vane. It's Jonah's cabin. The outside light's still on. It tells her she's going the wrong way.

A dog barks. Then it's right there beside her, nudging her. *Whose dog is this? They should keep it in their yard.* He barks again and she realizes he knows where the shore is and is trying to lead her there. But when she attempts to follow she moves too quickly. Her feet slip, she falls. It hurts her head so much.

The world has turned upside down. Lilly is forgetting again. *I am on the river. I am on the ice.* She hears a distant crack and this time it scares her. Pain in her head, and the tiredness, too. "George," she calls. He will come for her, he always has. They are tethered to each other by an invisible cord that has had many years to strengthen and it can't be broken now. "George!"

Only silence.

She looks up at the darkening sky. She's so cold, too cold, but hot at the same time. This must be how Virginia felt. It's clear, this thought. It brings her back, frightens her, but also comforts her. Better this, better here. No fluorescent hospital-room lights. No disappointed eyes.

I loved you so much, Virginia. I tried.

She thinks about their bedroom, her and George's: matching lamps, books on the bedside tables, the old flip clock with its moving numbers, the clicking slide of the past, a sound she and George had grown used to. Better this, maybe, than going on the way she is. Better to go now than to forget it all and leave George and Mae to gather up her pieces.

The sky is black but stars float across it like flecks of salt from a shaker. The dog is gone, whatever his name is. A star above her grows larger. She fears it might consume her, but then a peace begins to steal over her. She still wishes she didn't have to go, still wishes for more time, but she also understands. She *understands*. She's leaving and she won't be able to come back. But that doesn't mean the people she loves will never follow. Lilly closes her eyes and feels only relief.

Have a brandy.

It will warm you from the inside out. (But only one:
it's never good to overindulge on the hard stuff. Yes,
Mom. I know I'm not old enough to drink yet, but I
know what I know.)

It ends: all kisses must. Gabe pulls away first and wishes he hasn't as soon as he has, but he needs to look at her. Those eyes, that hair, that skin. "Hi." If her hair wasn't full of snow, he would wonder if there had ever been a storm. He sees the taillights of the bus down the road, the old-fashioned streetlamp in front of a spindly tree that doesn't look like it will survive winter, the blanketed parking lot. It surprises him, all of it. For a moment he had thought they were somewhere else.

"Hi," she says in return.

"How have you been?" There's a growing distance in her eyes. She's thinking about something else.

"That's a big question, to cover... How many years has it been?" she says.

"Seventeen," he replies, too quickly.

"Seventeen," she repeats.

"Lilly mentioned something's going on with you. With your life."

Mae nods. "A broken engagement," she says. "And I'm better off." She brushes some of the snow from her hair. "And you?"

"Recent divorce. Better off, too." He feels an urgent need

to tell her everything and to know everything. What if they never get anything more than this moment? What if she disappears into the night again, changes her mind? But he forces himself to be patient.

"Lilly said George called you. About your father."

"Yes, he did call. It made me happy, to hear his voice. So I came. And you were here, too." He smiles. There's a lightness in his chest.

She breathes out, a silken cloud that hangs in the air. "George isn't living at the inn right now. Things aren't good. I'm worried. I don't know what to do. And my grandmother—" She's shaking, and he doesn't know if she's cold, but he thinks she might be scared, so he pulls her to him again. She looks up. "I've never seen her like that. It was horrible. It didn't seem like her, not at all."

"Do you want to go back?" He doesn't. He wants to wait right there for another bus, and then they can go away together.

"Yes. I need to talk to Lilly, and do you think you could go to The Ship and talk to George? Please? Tell him we need him, tell him to come home? Tell him I'm worried about Lilly, tell him whatever you have to tell him, just get him to come home. If *you* can come home after all this time—then he can. Then he can get over whatever it is that has happened and get back to the inn."

They part in front of The Ship. Gabe watches her walk away. He doesn't move. He's not afraid to go in and talk to George, he just needs time to think. Finally, he turns and looks at the building: neat siding painted gray with white trim, a white sign with a picture of a red ship hanging out front. A mix of optimism and desolation; a motel in a tourist town in the middle of winter is one of the loneliest places in the world, but summer does always come.

He walks toward the building and imagines his father staying here. Instead of a hospital bed, he can picture him here in this place. He tries now to think of one good memory of his father, just one. Jonah wasn't always raging, drunk, filthy, swearing, hitting, hurting—was he? But he did do those things enough times that they've blurred all the calmer moments away, the moments when he and Gabe might have sat together at the kitchen table, eating soup or chili or whatever it was Jonah had dumped out of a can that night. And he had taught Gabe to fish, how to bait a hook and drill a hole in the ice and "think like a muskie." And sometimes, if they were out ice fishing, there would be a few moments before Jonah was entirely drunk when Gabe had even been able pretend that they were just a normal father and son, out on the ice together in Half Moon Bay.

Inside, the clerk, who looks vaguely familiar, calls George's room, then tells Gabe to go ahead. Unit 12. Gabe knocks, waits. The door opens.

"You came."

For the first moment, Gabe focuses on George's eyes. It's jarring to see a person after almost twenty years. Change is inevitable, and George was never young to Gabe, but he's an old, old man now. It strikes a chord of fear in Gabe's heart.

"The hospital called, not too long ago, about your father," George says. "Is that why you're here? I'm sorry, son."

That memory, so fresh in his mind, of fishing with his father—Gabe feels like he's been punched. "He's gone?"

"Yes. They couldn't find you. He was alone when he died." There's a sadness passing over George's face that Gabe doesn't know what to do with. Because how could anyone, and especially George Summers, grieve for Jonah Broadbent, how could anyone who saw what he had done to Gabe over the years care if he died alone? The sucker-punch feeling is gone already, replaced with only anger, then numbness. It's over, Jonah is dead, Gabe is finally free—and he didn't have to sit there not wanting to hold his father's cold hand, not knowing what to feel, or when the right time would be to get up and leave.

George opens the door wide. "Come in and we'll talk more," he says, turning and heading down the narrow hallway, which leads to a room with a double bed covered in a green-and-burgundy-flowered polyester duvet. At Summers' Inn, each room had a theme—Wildflower, Riverview, Garden, Rosebud. Gabe always stayed in the Riverview, which had simple blue-and-white decor and the best view. He never understood why they gave him the room with the best view.

There's a chair at a battered writing desk and George pulls it out for Gabe, then sits on the bed.

"The nurse called because I'm the one who brought him in. I spent a little time with your father recently. We were both staying here and he was in need. To be honest, so was I. Your father loved you, you know. He did. I know he hurt you, but he loved you. He would spend time in your room, he told me. He was sleeping in there toward the end. He missed you. He thought of you until his mind went and he couldn't."

Gabe focuses on a stain on the carpet to the left of George's chair leg.

"All right," George finally says. "I understand. Maybe we can talk about him another time."

Gabe can look up again. "What are you doing in this place? And what will it take to get you to go back home?"

"It's not something I want to talk about."

"Maybe I can help."

George shakes his head. "No one can help."

"Mae is home," Gabe says. "She's the one who sent me here. I was just with her. She wants you home, too. She needs you."

"I know. I got the message she left with the front desk. But her being here is even more reason for me to stay away."

"I don't understand."

"*I* don't understand a lot of things," George says, and Gabe realizes he's talking about something else now. He wants an explanation from Gabe, he must. Lilly told him the same thing, that he stole the money, and when George looks at Gabe he sees a thief. Gabe tries to hang on to the feeling he had on the train platform with Mae, that feeling of absolution. He can't tell Lilly's lie to George, not now, not when Mae asked him to bring George home. "I'm sorry" is all he can say.

"No, no. Don't. It's all right. It was a long time ago. We would have given you the money, you know. I was always sure Lilly felt that way, too, though we never talked about it."

"Yeah. Thanks."

The phone rings, startling both of them. George reaches for the receiver.

"Hello?"

Gabe can hear Mae's voice from where he's sitting. "Grandpa?"

"Mae," George says. "What is it?"

"I can't find Grandma."

*T*he cabin smells like spilled liquor and mildew and failure to thrive. A black garbage bag spills its contents onto the kitchen floor.

"Jonah?" Virginia calls. A groan. She follows the sound to the living room. He's facedown on the couch, an empty bottle on the up- ended milk crate beside him. She shakes him, hard, "Jonah, Chase took out the hovercraft and didn't come back, and now it's raining and getting warmer and the ice isn't safe and— Oh, wake up, come on! I need you to take me out in your ice cutter to find him. Or give me the keys. Where are the keys, Jonah?"

She shakes him again and he mutters, "Tell the boy to stay away as long as he wants, I don't care. How many times do I have to hit him before he gets it and just goes?"

Gabe, poor Gabe. She's going to adopt Gabe herself, she decides then and there. Right after she finds Chase. "Where are the keys to your cutter, Jonah?"

"Aw, fuck off, will you?"

She looks for the keys herself. Sticky patches on the counters, old newspapers, flyers, opened cans of stew, half of them still full and stinking, the flotsam and jetsam of a wasted life: matchbooks, lottery tickets, expired coupons.

Back in the kitchen, she picks up the phone and hears only dead air. *"Pay your goddamn phone bill! I hate you!"* she shouts. But it isn't true: hating Jonah would be like hating a wounded animal. And also, she can't. Could never. She still has memories of him as someone else. A friend, and a true one.

She slams the door as she leaves the cabin. She slides across the dock and looks for the keys in the cutter, but they aren't there. It's raining harder than she can remember it raining, ever; she's soaked to her underclothes.

She's on the river again, no choice. She's running across the ice. It feels soft. There's a layer of water over the ice now, but it still holds her. It's not too late. It's never too late. Virginia thinks of Mae, safe in the attic of the inn with Gabe, playing pirates. *"Be brave, always."* Virginia runs. For Chase, but also for Mae. Her love swells, surprises her, delights her, terrifies her. It is because of this love that Virginia believes harder. It is because of this love that Virginia presses on, determined that she will not give up, no matter how hard it rains, that she will live to teach her daughter to do the same.

PART TWO

---

*Make newspaper boats and look for puddles outside
to float them in, or head to the creek.
This is a terrific family activity that will distract you
from the rain.*

In the basement of the church, there are half a dozen women Lilly's age. They bustle back and forth with sandwich trays. Their low heels clack on the polished concrete floor. Mae takes off her coat and hangs it on a wire hanger near the door. She's wearing a black jersey dress she bought the day before. She knows she'll never wear this dress again.

She arrived with George but he has allowed himself to be led away by the women. She watches him go. Did he always shuffle like that? She stands beside the coat rack with its row of wire hangers now empty, and imagines them full, soon, with the coats of Lilly's friends, all come to mourn her. Because Lilly is dead. Mae lifts her hand. She wants to call her grandfather back. But he's already gone.

"Tea?" One of the women has materialized beside her, leads her away from the empty coat rack and those sad, guilty thoughts. A warm foam cup is pressed into her hand.

"Thank you," Mae murmurs. Maybe it will help with the nausea that is now a constant companion, as if her grief were manifesting itself in physical illness. She leaves the basement and walks upstairs, where she finds George in the sanctuary with the minister, holding his own cup of tea. The minister pats Mae's shoulder when she approaches.

"The flowers look nice," Mae lies. They don't; they're depressing. Too many lilies, which she knows her grandmother hated because of the overpowering funereal smell. But people probably just assumed, because of her name, that lilies would be nice. People inevitably do the wrong thing in situations like this. But is there a right thing? You can't bring a person back when they're gone.

Reverend Judith is wearing a robe and a necklace with a wooden cross. "God has a plan for us all," she says to George, and Mae finds herself abruptly baffled. God's plan was that Lilly would fall and hit her head, hard, on a frozen river, that without her family to help her it would be too late by the time they got her to the hospital? God's plan was that she would hide the truth from them, in so many ways, and then leave them before they could make peace with her, and with one another? God's plan was that Mae would regret, for the rest of her life, running off down that driveway instead of staying home and talking to Lilly, telling her that no matter what she did, she loved her anyway? Because it's true now: she loves her anyway, and so she should have loved her anyway when she was alive, no matter what revelations she brought forth. She lost a child; she lost her daughter. What Lilly had done was wrong, but she had suffered and never said anything about it to Mae. All these years, Mae had assumed she was the one who suffered most from the loss of her parents. Not true.

Reverend Judith is saying something to Mae, but Mae is looking at her grandfather. *Did* you *love her anyway?* she wants to ask him. *How could you have left her alone like that?*

"Mae?"

"Pardon me, can you repeat that?" Mae says to the reverend.

"I said, you'll speak first. Are you all right with that, delivering your eulogy first? And then we'll do another hymn, and I've prepared a short homily, and one of the women from the Ladies' Society wants to say something."

"Oh. That's fine. Could you excuse me? I just need to…"

Outside the sanctuary, she hears the side door of the church open, hears heels clicking across the floor. It's Viv. "Darling, how are you holding up?" Viv smells, as always, of rosewater and Yardley talcum powder and rouge from a pot. "Where is your grandfather?"

"In there." Mae indicates the sanctuary. People are starting to file in and this panics her. "I'll meet you in there, I just need a second."

Viv nods and says, "Of course you do, of course. Poor baby. Do you want me to…?"

"No, thanks. I just need to be alone." She opens the first door she sees and finds herself in the nursery.

She still doesn't know what to say. She had thought it would come to her as the days passed, but nothing has. All of Lilly's and George's friends will be disappointed when she speaks. She will be a letdown to everyone.

She wants more tea, maybe some ginger ale. She has a tissue in her hand, crumpled, and she presses it against her face. It doesn't help.

The door to the room opens. She looks up.

Gabe. He'd been in town, at a meeting he couldn't cancel, something about his father's affairs, but had promised he'd be there in time for the start of the funeral. "Sorry I'm late."

"You're not." Gabe is holding a box of tissues. An entire box. Mae imagines that Lilly would say something like, "Bless you," to him. She doesn't say that. He sits down beside her.

"So, why are you hiding in here?"

She blows her nose. "Because I didn't write the eulogy. I'm such an idiot."

"It's a tough thing to have to do. Just tell them you can't."

"My name is already in the order of service."

"I'm sure everyone will understand."

"Lilly won't," Mae says. She's been making a point of speaking of Lilly in the past tense but it feels better not to. "What am I supposed to say about her, if I didn't really know her?"

"Of course you knew her. You just didn't know everything about her. Say what you feel."

"That would be disastrous. Hi, everyone, I feel horrible. I'm the worst granddaughter and person in the world. The end."

"You're not a bad person. You're a great person." He puts his arm around her shoulders and pulls her to him for a second, but it feels like a friendly gesture. Since that night on the train platform, there hasn't been any more kissing. He held her hand a lot as they sat by Lilly's bedside, as they made their decisions and waited, but it's all a blur to Mae.

"Do you remember when I was a kid, and sometimes I would just start to cry for no reason? And Lilly would take me upstairs if the crying got really bad?"

"Yeah. And I'd sit in the lobby, worrying. Waiting."

"Worrying about what?"

He's silent for a moment. Then he says, "It was worse when it rained. On rainy days, you were always more likely to be like that. I would try to distract you."

The organ music begins to play in the sanctuary. It vibrates through the soles of her feet on the floor and moves up through her body. She stands, but she doesn't go anywhere.

"I'm angry," she says. "I'm really, really angry."

"She's not here now. There's no point in being angry at her."

"I'm not angry at her, I'm angry at my grandfather. I can hardly look at him."

Gabe stands, too. He takes both her hands in his. "Don't be," he says. "It won't do you any good. It was no one's fault, what happened to Lilly. You have to let it go."

She pulls her hands away, afraid that soon her aimless anger will be directed at him. "I should really get in there." She makes her way with Gabe into the sanctuary, where everyone has gathered. She sits beside George, and before she can say anything, Gabe files into another pew nearby. She wishes she could tell him she wanted him to sit beside her. She tips the tissue box toward George but he shakes his head as the organ music reaches a crescendo, then stops. When Reverend Judith says it's time to pray, Mae bows her head, closes her eyes, sees bright lights and spots and darkness.

Amen.

It's her turn to speak. She stands, approaches the podium, clears her throat. "Um," she says into the microphone. It echoes. "My grandmother was…"

She was what? She was a good person? She took in a boy who wasn't her own, and treated him like a son, then kicked him out and pretended he stole money? And all because she never got over losing her daughter? She used to look you all in the face and pretend she was fine, but all this time, she was suffering and you didn't know.

"My grandmother and my grandfather were…"

They were what? They were married for sixty-seven years, but then had a fight that ripped them apart. I have no idea what it was about.

"I'm sorry," she says, too close to the microphone; this time the feedback makes the congregation wince as a collective. Hands reach up to adjust hearing aids. "I can't. I can't do this. I didn't know her, really. I didn't know them. I thought I did, but I didn't, and I just— You didn't either." She looks at her grandfather again, but George isn't looking at her. He's staring up at a spot behind her, at Christ on the cross. She tries again. "I loved her. But I don't know what else to say. I'm sorry." She steps down from the podium and walks out of the sanctuary.

Talk to someone.
A stranger, a friend, a loved one.
And when they talk to you, really listen.

First, silence. Then noise moves through the room like a gentle wave. Throats clear. There are whispers. Rustling papers. Reverend Judith approaches the podium Mae has just abandoned and begins to speak about loss and recovery, about being supportive of our brothers and our sisters as they move through their grief. Gabe remembers how he always hated church. "Let's sing," she says. "This was one of Lilly's favorites. Hymn number 186 in the red book."

Hands reach for hymnals, the organ music begins, Gabe hears the woman behind him start to sing loudly: "'On a hill far away stood an old rugged cross, / the emblem of suffering and shame…'"

He stands and strides down the center aisle with his eyes on the door. Later, over sandwiches in the church basement, people will say, *Did you see how he took the hymnal with him? Who would steal a hymnal?* He tosses the hymnal on a back pew; he didn't mean to take it. He hates this town, he really does—and yet, when he's outside on the steps of the church and he sees Mae shake her head, when flakes of snow fall out of her hair and they're lit up by the sun so it looks like she's shaking out fragments of sunlight, he doesn't hate anything anymore.

The door he has opened spills the singing out into the afternoon. "'So I'll cherish the old rugged cross, / till my trophies at last I lay down…'"

"What did she like about this hymn?" Mae says. "She wasn't all that religious, was she? We didn't pray before meals, didn't talk about God. But she went to church, and she made my mom go, and she made me go, and you had to go sometimes, too. And she loved this particular hymn, but now I'll never know why."

"I bet she liked it because it was firm, because it stood for something. That was her, don't you think? Rugged, in her way. In the ways that she could be. Strong."

"She suffered."

"Everyone does."

"She suffered more than most people."

"She's gone. She's not suffering anymore."

"She's gone," Mae repeats. She looks so sad; he wants to fix it. Why did he say that, that Lilly is gone? She knows that. She feels bad enough about it.

"I love you." *What?* He's blurted it out; now he tries not to panic. But it makes her smile; he gets his reward.

"Thank you," she says, stepping closer to him, putting her arms around his waist and her head on his chest, as if this were something she does all the time.

He laughs quietly. "Okay. Sure. You're welcome." He waits for that familiar feeling to steal its way in. That sensation of inadequacy, the urge to run. It doesn't come. He's exactly where he wants to be.

There's organ music inside again. He holds her until the church bells begin their lonely, singular chime, staccato reminders of the shortness of life, the fact of endings. But Mae here in his arms, it feels like a beginning. Is it right to feel such joy in the midst of so much pain? He's never felt hope like this before, never in his life, or at least not in the one he had after she was gone. He's not sure what to do with it but he sure as hell isn't going to run away from it. He holds her tighter.

The church door opens. George is there, blinking in the sunlight like a newborn. He's carrying the urn. Lilly. Mae pulls away from Gabe, and Gabe says, "I'm sorry," to George because that's what you say to people at funerals, isn't it? Mae doesn't say anything.

"I had to leave," George says. "There's supposed to be a reception, sandwiches, more tea and we're supposed to...talk to people. But I can't." His voice is like a gravel road when it used to be a smooth comfort. "The ladies will come out looking for us soon. We'd better go."

Gabe takes a step back from Mae and prepares to say good-bye to them, because this is not his place, this is their loss, not his but George reaches for him. "Gabe, could you please drive?" He tucks the urn under one arm for a moment while he hands Gabe the car keys.

Mae has her hand on his arm, too. They're flanking him, leading him away from the church. "Let's go home," she says.

The reflex feeling has arrived, and it's almost a relief. Gabe's heart rate accelerates and he finds himself starting to think of excuses. *I can't take care of people. I can't do this.* But maybe he can. Maybe he has to. Because he loves these people. And he loved Lilly, even though she hurt him. He loved her because he understood what it meant to be wounded, and to inflict wounds in return.

He takes George's elbow so he can hold him steady over a patch of ice. He opens the car door for Mae. He drives George's old Buick slowly, as if the two people he were transporting are ill and must be handled with extreme care. George holds the urn in his lap and Mae stares out the window the whole way home, keeps her eyes on the river. Who knows what she sees out there? Ghosts, from the look on her face. Ghosts, everywhere. He'll save her from them, and George, too. New York feels very far away. Once, he thought he'd never go back to Alexandria Bay. Now he can't imagine ever leaving.

Build something.
There are tools and scrap wood in the shed.
And, yes, bandages and ice in the kitchen, in case
you accidentally hammer your finger.

George is getting a mug from the cupboard when the door, which has been hanging askew for some time, falls off altogether, crashes to the floor and misses his foot by an inch.

Mae runs into the kitchen in a robe, a towel wrapped around her head. Her face is shiny, scrubbed clean; she looks like her mother. "Shhh," Mae says to the dog, who is barking idiotically at the fallen cupboard door. Then, "Oh. I've been meaning to fix that. Did you get hurt?" But she doesn't look at him, not directly. Mae won't look at him anymore, George has noticed.

"I'm fine, don't worry, go get dressed."

He takes the empty mug and sits at the table, stares at the wall obstinately. He's an old man, but he can play at her game, too. She's not the only one suffering.

He hears Mae sigh. It's not just the physical resemblance: she's like Virginia in so many ways, though she doesn't seem to know it. He should tell her. He should tell her a lot of things. He should not be acting this way; he should apologize. But he hears her leave the kitchen. Too late.

The dog is nosing his leg. It makes him uncomfortable, so angry at the unwanted touch he feels it prickling his skin like an itch. He pets the dog because otherwise he thinks he might hit it. He stops, to test himself, and his hand curls into a fist as if it has a will of its own.

Gabe comes in just in time. George resumes his patting of the dog. He scratches behind his ears, even murmurs, "Good boy." Very convincing. He tries to smile at Gabe. He's trying to get used to having him around, but it's not like it used to be, when the boy lived here. George took care of Gabe, once; now it's the other way around. And so much has changed. Gabe is a man now, and George is a very old one. Looking at Gabe reminds George of the passage of time. He has almost nothing left. He has lost it all. The smile, which was unsuccessful in the first place, fades.

"Oops." Gabe has seen the cupboard door. "I'll go get the drill. You okay? Did anyone get hurt?"

"Just leave it."

"It won't take much." Gabe feels around on the ground for the screws, finds them and puts them on the counter. "I'll do it in a minute. Let me just get this stuff into the fridge. I'm no chef, but I make a mean grilled cheese. I have a secret ingredient. A tiny bit of sugar. It caramelizes things." George thinks he's supposed to try to smile again, because Gabe has told him this as if sharing an important confidence. He doesn't. But Gabe refuses to be deterred from his quest to cheer up George. He's been at it for days. "Or—" he holds up a frozen food box, the kind Lilly said they should never buy because the salt content would give them hypertension "—there's lasagna. Which do you feel like?"

"Anything is fine. Thank you." George stands. "I think I'll go upstairs and lie down."

"Sure. I'll let you know when dinner's ready. How about lasagna, then? Comfort food?"

"Whatever you think."

George is keeping the urn on the top shelf of his closet, but when he reaches for it to put it back on the bed, he feels cold metal instead of smooth ceramic: his old ditty box. He leaves Lilly where she is, takes the box down, puts it on the bed.

When he opens it, right there is the photograph. He holds it and looks into her eyes. "What if he hadn't died? What then, Lilly?" The shirts and sweaters hanging there in the closet look like dead, defeated things. "But he did die," George says. "I remember every minute of it, and every moment after. Our life—sometimes it passed by us so fast hundreds of days blurred into one. Did you feel that way? But then there are some days that still feel like yesterday. The bad days and the best days, especially. Don't you agree?" He sits down on the bed, still holding the photograph. There's one day that's so vivid he's in it now, just recalling it. His bad day and his best day, all rolled into one.

George moved as quickly as he could down the side streets of Alexandria Bay with his limp—a wound from the depth charges that had gone off as the boat went down, a wound that would heal and had not even required hospitalization, which was why he had been given the terrible task of delivering the news of Everett's death to his friend's parents.

They were waiting on the front porch of the inn, as if they had known he was coming. They stood together and came to meet him. They leaned on one another, a triangle of support.

He talked with Everett's parents for a while, tried to be as gentle as he could with the details. Then Everett's father went inside to get Vivian. That was the worst part, telling Viv her brother was gone. She beat her fists against George's chest and said, "Why didn't you stop him, why didn't you do something?" Just when George thought he couldn't take it anymore, she dropped to the steps and folded in upon herself.

Eventually, there was silence as the afternoon started to turn golden. The four of them sat and watched the light and thought about Everett. Probably, they thought about how he would never again see the light change like this. For his part, George remembered the afternoon his mother died of cancer, when he was ten. Everett came over to his house and knocked on the door. He had two fishing poles with him. He said, like he always did, "Wanna go try 'n' catch a big one?" His eyes were sad but his voice was bright, a lifeline for George in the darkness of this unutterably sad childhood moment.

"Someone needs to tell Lilly," said Catharine, Everett's mother, when the light was almost gone.

"She's living in Watertown," said Vivian, her voice listless. "She's working at a factory, like a man. She said I should do it, too, join the war effort, and I thought about it, but—" She held out a pale manicured hand and smiled at him with broken eyes.

Later, Vivian went inside to get him the address of the rooming house. "Do you want to come?" he asked her. She shook her head. He patted her shoulder, shook Everett's father's hand, hugged Catharine and left.

First, he went back home. He went to his father's desk and took the ring that was once his mother's. Then he drove to Watertown.

At the rooming house door, the landlady regarded him suspiciously, but let him in and called for Lilly. They sat in the parlor because male guests were not allowed upstairs. The curtains were closed and the feeble light of a dark-shaded lamp lit up only one corner of the room.

She didn't say anything when he told her. She sat very still, staring at the tiny shaft of light the lamp was casting on the opposite wall as the darkness gathered in the rest of the room.

George studied her, trying to put his finger on what was different. A slight fullness of face, and, yes, when he glanced down he could see that her midsection was thicker. How could Everett not have mentioned, during those cold, dark, rough nights belowdecks, that he and Lilly had...

But maybe it wasn't true. Maybe he was just imagining it. If she were pregnant, she would tell him. If she were pregnant, what would that mean?

"How?" she asked him, her eyes now bright with unshed tears. "How, exactly?"

He tried to explain it, but never managed to. "Everett is a hero. He saved so many of our men from drowning. Just not himself. He even went back for a dog, our ship's mascot." This felt disloyal, telling her this. He hadn't mentioned it to Everett's parents, and knew he never would tell them. He would also never tell anyone how he had screamed at his friend, how his last words to him were, *Goddamn you! Come back here, goddamn you, don't be a fool!* "The dog lived. The survivors wanted to give it to Everett's parents as a gift. I told them to keep it, give it to a kid who had lost his dad or something."

"A dog?" That was what did it. She covered her face and started to sob.

All he could do was watch her cry. Eventually, she stopped and put her hands on that tiny swell of her stomach and he found himself mesmerized, fearful, intrigued. But it was just for a moment, and then her hands were gone and he thought he must have imagined it, the whole thing. She'd gained a little weight, was all.

George took his mother's ring from his pocket. He didn't get down on one knee; it didn't seem like the right thing to do. He said, "I'll take care of you."

"I know you will." She crossed her arms over her belly, hugging herself.

"I love you."

"Thank you, George," she said.

Gabe is tapping at George's bedroom door and saying supper is ready.

"I'll be down in just a moment." He's unable to keep the irritation out of his voice. He stares out the window, down at his car. And an idea comes to him. He's a free man, isn't he? He can go where he wants.

The dog is waiting just outside the bedroom door. As he shuffles downstairs, the infernal thing follows, his own personal albatross, at his heels.

In the kitchen, Mae is sitting at the table and Gabe is pulling the lasagna out of the oven. The table has been set and a salad has been tossed; there are tumblers full of ice water; a checked napkin is folded beside each plate. Gabe has moved so effortlessly back into their lives. George watches him and wonders. Can he trust him, to keep Mae safe?

"I hope you're hungry," Gabe says, holding up a serving spoon.

"I'm not, actually. Please just give me a very small serving."

"Me, too," says Mae. She stands and pours food into the dog's dish, refreshes his water.

"No problem." Gabe has cut a large slice, but he pushes that plate aside and cuts two smaller ones. "There's bread and salad, too."

George can't imagine eating anything. He notices Mae has pushed her lasagna aside and is picking at her salad.

"You should eat," George says to her, man of the house once more. A vain attempt. She puts down her fork. Virginia

in her eyes again: quiet courage, a durability. And resentment. *Now I've done it.*

"I should eat?" she says.

George nods. He should have just stayed upstairs.

"Don't you think you could have worried about Grandma
a little, maybe, instead of me? Don't you think that instead
of leaving her over some fight you two had, you could have
stayed, and maybe noticed she wasn't doing well, and if you
had, maybe she wouldn't have—"

George pushes his chair back. His fork clatters to the floor.

"No! Don't you dare go upstairs and hide again. *I'll* go."
These are commands, and George accepts them. He doesn't
move until Mae disappears through the swinging door. The
dog follows her, thank God.

"I'm sorry," Gabe says. "I'm trying to make this normal,
like a regular family dinner, but obviously I don't know what
that is and it's probably too soon."

"It's not you," George says. "It's me. Everything is because of me."

"What do you mean?"

"I can't. I can't tell anyone."

"Can't tell anyone what? Can't tell anyone why?"

He considers Gabe's words. "When Lilly was alive, I was
keeping the secret because I was waiting until I'd calmed
down enough to talk to her about it myself. Too late for that
now."

Gabe looks alarmed. "Sit down. Please. It's all right, it
doesn't matter—"

"You have to promise me you won't tell Mae."

Gabe frowns. "I think she knows."

Chest pain. "She does? She knows that Virginia was not
my daughter?"

Now it's Gabe who sits. "What?"

George beckons for him to lean in. When Gabe is close enough, he speaks in a low voice.

"Virginia was not my daughter. Lilly hid this fact from me." These words hang in the room between them as if they've been written on a spiderweb. George wants to reach up his hands and bat them away, erase their existence. If only.

"What do you..." Then Gabe goes mute. George sees the boy in him again, the boy who would always retreat from them. It makes him nervous, but he's made his decision.

"Virginia wasn't mine," George repeats. The firm emphasis does not suture the wound. Only a fool could have believed it would.

"Then, who...?" Gabe begins, trails off. He doesn't want to know, George realizes. He doesn't want this burden.

"My friend Everett. We were in the navy together. We were best friends. Our ship went down. He drowned. He was Vivian's brother, and he was Lilly's first love. She wasn't mine, she was his first, and should have been his always. This place, too, it was supposed to be his. But his parents gave it to me because Viv didn't want it, she wanted to run off to Hollywood, and they couldn't bear to stay here. When Lilly and I were married and moved in here, she was already pregnant with his child, with Virginia, but she didn't mention it to me. Let us live our entire lives in a lie, until she let it slip one night. She never loved me, Lilly didn't. That's why I left. It wasn't some stupid fight, it wasn't what Mae thinks. That's why I was living at The Ship. Because she broke my heart." George opens and closes his mouth. He wants to say more, but he feels aphasic, like those poor people Lilly used to volunteer to sit with at the hospital. "Can you imagine that?" he finally does manage. "Not knowing the person you've lived with for sixty-seven years, and known your whole life before that?"

Gabe's expression changes, for just a second. But then it's gone, whatever it was.

"I think Mae needs to know this. She should know. If she understood why you and Lilly were apart—"

"Me over Lilly, is that what you're suggesting? I take back my dignity, I win back my granddaughter, by admitting to her that she isn't really mine, but I disgrace Lilly by revealing her deception? No. Don't let me down, Gabe. Don't tell her."

Gabe flinches, and George realizes what he's done—he's putting this between two people who should be left alone, free to fall in love again. And he's placing another burden on Gabe's shoulders. It's a cruelty the boy doesn't deserve. No matter what mistakes he made in the past George wants to say he's sorry as soon as the words are out. He sighs and reaches up but doesn't allow himself to touch Gabe. "You've been taking good care of us, and I want you to keep doing that. For Mae. But not for me. I need to leave here." He lets his hand fall back down to his lap.

"You don't—"

"Don't argue with me!" George's voice is harsh again. He stands, and it is revealed: he is small, he is fading away. But he cranes his neck and draws himself up to his full height, such as it is. Aching bones, aching heart. "Just take care of Mae. Promise me. Promise me now."

Gabe lowers his head, chastened. Time falls away. "I promise you."

"For heaven's sake, get out of the car!" But the dog doesn't move. "Fine, come along, you won't be happy."

George drives the few miles outside of town it takes to get to the Alexandria Bay Cemetery. When he gets there, he lets the dog out and Bud starts to run up and down the rows of graves. He walks through the silent rows, carrying the urn.

In the trunk, a small suitcase and Lilly's cedar box. He's taken nothing else. What else is there?

He pauses at Virginia's grave first. "Hello, girl," he says, as he always does, his voice breaking, as it always does. He wishes that instead of his sad offering he had flowers to leave in front of the stone that says "Gone Fishing"—little Mae's suggestion, all those years ago. "Maybe she'll come back." The hope in her eyes; George had never seen anything sadder. And sadder still was the fact that there was no monument there for her father, that Chase's cold and imperious family had arrived shortly after learning of their son's death and stayed only long enough to arrange for his body to be shipped back to Toronto and buried in the family plot there. Somewhere called Mount Pleasant—George had learned this and told Mae once. She had not had a perfect father, and Lilly never liked to speak of him, but George hadn't thought it was fair that Mae had never been given the chance to say goodbye, that there was nowhere she could go to try to make peace.

He opens the top of the urn and lifts out a handful of Lilly's ashes. He sprinkles them on Virginia's grave and they stain the snow an ugly gray black. *You were always so easy on her, on both of them.* Lilly said that once. It was the night Gabe left, when George tried to stop her from going to the boy's apartment to confront him. And she was right—he had been. He had always treated Virginia, and Mae, too, as if they were favorite nieces of his. Maybe he *had* always known, in his heart. And what does it matter? Any tie to them has been wrenched away from him. He has nothing.

He walks toward the military section of the graveyard. His feet are cold and damp. Perhaps he'll catch pneumonia and die. A futile hope. There, his flashlight lands on it: *Everett Patrick Green. November 29, 1917–September 20, 1941. Died in the service of God and country. Beloved son, brother and friend.*

He brushes snow away from the letters and numbers. "I was not a friend," he says to Everett. "I was your enemy, trying to steal the woman you loved. We both know I never would have succeeded, though, had you lived. If you had lived, everyone would have been better off. None of the bad things that happened ever would have happened. You would have made sure of it, you would have saved everyone."

He opens the lid of the urn again and turns it upside down. The wind blows some of the ashes over to other graves, and some of them hit Everett's gravestone, and some of them land where he wanted them to. It's not how he imagined it would be, but is anything?

"There. She's yours." He puts the urn down on the grave. He calls for the dog and returns to the car.

But when he opens the car door, the dog barks and hangs back. "Come on," he says. "You can't stay here." He whimpers but climbs in. George gets in and closes the door, then turns to put his gloves on the front seat. But he can't put them down. Because Lilly is sitting there.

"What have you done, George? Why on earth did you do that? And where do you think you're going?"

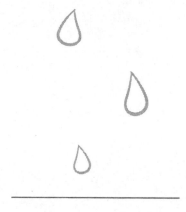

Watch a movie—maybe something creepy that goes
with the mood of the rainy gloom.

"Where did he say he was going?"

"He didn't."

"Why did you let him go?"

"I'm sorry." Gabe looks down, and his shoulders hunch for a moment before he straightens them. "I didn't know what he was going to do if I didn't let him."

"Damn it, Gabe! You needed to stop him! You needed to keep him here with us." She leaves the kitchen and storms down the hall, each footfall a tiny earthquake. She doesn't feel like an adult; she feels like the teenage girl she was the last time Gabe was in this house, and it's been happening more and more. She slams the front door and heads down the little hill toward the boathouse. Inside, it's dusty and damp. She walks to the far end of the boathouse and sits in the chair that is there. *I'm scared and I'm sad*, she should have said to Gabe. *I do need to be taken care of, just for now, until I can breathe again. I'm sorry I yelled at you, you don't deserve that.* Instead, she shoved him away. Lilly. George. And now Gabe. All the people she loves. But Gabe, he never stays. She knows this and needs to protect herself from it.

She looks around. Being in here reminds her of the day her parents died. She can remember it still, the way the day started, being awakened just before dawn by her parents arguing in the next room. The volume of the muffled voices had increased and Mae had stood and pressed her ear against the wall of her room, even though she'd been taught it wasn't polite to eavesdrop, that you could never listen against walls and doors when you lived at an inn.

"How could you?" she had heard her mother say.

"Virginia, come on. It was just a few beers with some of the guys. You can't expect me to not drink ever, can you?"

"Yes! Yes, I can. It's never *just a few beers* with you, Chase. It's never that, and you know it, and it's almost dawn, and you come stumbling in here! And you said you'd finally work on the cabin. But how can you do that now? You'll be sick, you'll be sleeping it off, the cabin's not going to be finished before the freeze, like you promised, we won't be able to spend the winter inside the cabin, finishing it off. You don't care about our plans, you don't care about our life, you only care about yourself!"

Their voices lowered. Eventually, there was silence. Mae went back to her bed and lay down and waited to see if they would start up again. They didn't. It took her a long time to fall asleep, but she finally did.

She woke again when it was light, and everything seemed just as it usually was. Her mother gave her an egg and toast for breakfast and told her she was going out to run errands and would be back later in the day. But Mae had a bad feeling in the pit of her stomach from the fighting. She threw the food away when her mother left the kitchen, threw away the last thing her mother ever gave her to eat. Gabe was supposed to come over that day, so Mae went outside to catch a glimpse of him crossing the river in the cutter, the one Jonah used to get back and forth from his forsaken island when the ice started to come in, or go out.

The river was empty, but she could see her father in the boathouse, moving around. She climbed down the bank. It was slippery. All the early snow they'd had was almost gone.

"Daddy?" she called, but he mustn't have heard her. He was sitting at the back of the boathouse on a chair now. He lifted something to his mouth and drank. A brown bottle. Beer.

"Daddy!" she shouted. She startled him. He dropped the bottle and it smashed on the ground. The smell hit her nostrils and she shouted again. "Mama said you weren't supposed to drink that."

"It's none of your business," her father snapped. Tears sprang to her eyes. He saw and came toward her. "Listen, Mac-flower, Daddy's really sorry. You're right, I shouldn't be drinking that, you're right, Mama said I shouldn't. Don't cry, baby. I'm really sorry." And he lifted her up and wrapped her in his arms. She was thinking that maybe if she got angry the way her mother did, he would actually stop, finally, and then there would be no more fighting. But she couldn't. She buried her face in his chest instead.

He put her down. "It'll be better. I promise. Why don't you run along now and let Daddy get some work done? It'll be okay."

She went inside, but she stopped at the window and watched him go off in the hovercraft. She had known it wasn't right, hadn't she? Even as a child, she had to have known that when someone had been drinking as heavily as he had been, all night and in the morning, too, you didn't let that person operate a boat. But she did nothing to stop him.

The door creaks open. Gabe. Mae can't decipher the look on his face. His expression is intense; he's got to be angry. She stands. She wants to say what he came to say to her first, she wants to beat him to it.

"We can't do this. Not now, not ever. The guy I was sup-posed to marry, he was a really bad guy. He did some horrible things, and I did them, too. Not on purpose—but still. I'm not who you remember. I'm not the person you think I am. I'm not that girl anymore. When you find that out, you're not going to want to know me."

"You haven't changed as much as you think. And whatever this guy made you do—" Gabe closes his eyes for a moment "—Jesus, is it wrong that I have the sudden desire to mur-der this guy? But, listen, whatever he made you do, it wasn't your fault. You're still a good person."

She shakes her head. "The person you knew never would have let any of these things happen. Lilly, George—*I* was supposed to take care of *them*. Now she's dead, he's run away and I did all that."

"You can't hold yourself responsible for things like this. You of all people should know that. You're the one who taught me that. Think about what you said, that night at the bus depot."

"It's different. You were just a kid. I'm supposed to be an adult. And I do things like this, I just do."

"It's okay to make mistakes. And sometimes, bad things just happen."

"I can't make this mistake, I can't make the next one I'm going to make, the one that has to do with you and me. I need you too much. That's not good."

"Why?"

"Because whenever I need someone, they—"

"I'm not going anywhere."

"You're always going somewhere, Gabe. You were always *going*. Across the river, out of my life… You can say right now that you aren't going anywhere, but it's just a matter of time before you see that I'm right, that everything I'm saying is right, and then you'll be gone, too."

"George will be back soon," he says. "You'll see. And everything will start to feel better. Meanwhile, I'm here. I'm not leaving. Don't push me away."

"I care about you so much. You know I do." He looks so happy, for just a second. It makes her wish she hadn't said it, except she doesn't think she would have been able to keep it in, knowing it would be her last chance to say it to him. She almost said more. "And it's too late for us. Friends. We could be friends again. But friends only."

Gabe takes two steps toward her, then stops. "No," he says.

"No?" she repeats.

"I can't do it again. I won't. I'm not saying we should jump into something. I know our history, I know a lot of shit is going on right now." He rubs the stubble on his chin. "I just got a divorce. You and this guy…" He clenches and unclenches a fist.

"Gabe—"

"There's nothing you can ever do or say or reveal that's going to make me stop loving you. Nothing. You can sit around blaming yourself for whatever you want to blame yourself for—I'm always going to just love you. I love you. So let me."

I love you. She now takes two steps toward him. "I love you, too," she says, and it's such a relief. She's lived beside a river long enough, lost enough to it, to know that when someone offers you a lifeline, you take it. And being told that she is loved by someone, just loved, always, she's been waiting for that since that morning in the boathouse, the moment before she lost almost everything. "How are we going to do this?"

"I was thinking about it: I'll take you on dates—adult dates where we go out for dinner and get to know each other again and don't sleep together at the end of it. No rushing."

She smiles; she can't help it now. She allows her heart to feel what it wants. She lets herself feel safe and hopes she can make this feeling last. "Okay," she says.

"Really?" He grins.

"Maybe we could go to Cavallario's. We could eat steak and discuss current events. Or stare awkwardly at each other. A legitimate first date."

He holds out his hand. "Tonight?"

She pictures the steak house, with its faux-castle exterior and dark interior. She imagines being there with Gabe. "Let's try it." She lets him lead her out of the boathouse, then stops.

"You'll stay?" she asks him. "You'll stay here for a while, at the inn? You won't go anywhere?"

"We haven't even had our first date, and you're asking me to move in?" But he pulls her close, and the rest of what he says is muffled by her hair against his lips. "I'm staying. Please believe me when I say I can't leave you again."

Get on the Great Lakes Seaway Trail and drive.

You'll find your way back.

George has been driving for two days. But Lilly hasn't returned to him, not yet. The night in the cemetery, sitting in the car, he gawked at her sitting there until finally he took a chance and spoke.

"Lilly? Is it really you?"

"Of course it's really me. What have you done, George, why did you throw my ashes on his grave?"

He was in mourning, he told himself, in shock. And this was an invention of his mind. And you don't talk to ghosts. But he couldn't help himself, the anger still seething, even now. "You're his, Lilly. Now it's official."

She shook her head. "First of all, I'm my own. I don't belong to anyone, not even you. And second, I certainly do not belong in a clump of snow in a lonely graveyard. You really don't know me at all, do you? Vivian is right. Men are useless."

George marveled at her lovely white hair. Lilly was just as pretty as she got older, maybe even more so.

"Did you ever listen to me, George? Did you ever hear a thing I said, our entire lives?"

"Of course I did. I—"

"If you had ever seen me, then you would know how much I loved you."

"The first time I ever told you I loved you, do you remember what you said?"

She lifts her chin. "I said thank you."

"You didn't tell me you loved me back, because you didn't yet."

"Oh, but I did. I thought you knew that—I thought what you didn't know was how grateful I was to you, how deeply grateful. It was important to me for you to know that."

"I saw you! The other night, I saw your face when you were looking at that photo of him!"

"I was losing my mind, damn it! Don't you see, can't you see, even now, what was happening to me?"

And then he could—he could see. What he had missed and what he had lost as a result. He put his face in his hands. "I'm sorry," he whispered. "I'm so very sorry."

But when he peered at the front seat through his fingers, she was gone. "Come back!" he shouted. The only response was the dog whining in the back seat, frightened by the sight of George sitting there, shouting at nothing. He started the car. "I'm going," he said. "You can't stop me." But even that didn't make her return.

Go scuba diving and check out one of the many shipwrecks lurking below the surface of our river. Who cares if it's raining? You'll already be wet.

In the Riverview Room, where Gabe is sleeping—just like he did when he was a kid—he imagines Mae in her own room, getting dressed for their date. He imagines her naked. He imagines walking down the hall and pushing open the door, but he doesn't do that, can't do that, and it is surely the hundredth time today he has had a thought like this. He said he wanted to take it slow, but he can hardly breathe when he's near her.

Now he goes to the bathroom to brush his teeth. She comes in and stands beside him and brushes her teeth, too. She's wearing a sweater and fitted jeans. Her hair is in a ponytail. He feels like they've been standing beside each other brushing their teeth in front of the mirror every day for years. He catches her eye. Her eyes crinkle up at the sides and she smiles with her toothbrush in her mouth and a little bit of toothpaste on her cheek. He likes what brushing their teeth before their date suggests: that there will be kissing later. He doesn't remember ever doing things like this with Natasha. She would go into the bathroom and close and lock the door when she was getting ready. She said the mystery was an important thing, but she didn't seem to have a contingency plan for when the enigmatic divide that existed between them became a chasm.

"See you downstairs," Mae says.

It's dusk. Mae is silent as they walk down the driveway together. He holds her hand and looks on either side of them, at the snow-piled cabins they used to play in, at the shed at the end of the drive with the lawnmower and the tools he would use when he was helping George with various tasks around the property. George called earlier, but they were out getting coffee. He left a message, no callback number. "Just checking in with you" was all he said. "Everything is fine, but I don't know when I'll be back." There were traffic sounds in the background, but no other clues. Mae went to her room after listening to the message, closed the door and came out a little later with red eyes. She said, "Do you think I should hire someone to try to find him?"

"Let's just give him a little more time," Gabe said, but he vowed to be there the next time George called. They needed to talk.

Gabe had made a reservation at the restaurant, but there was little point. The place is only half full. A waitress with ashy-blond hair, dark roots and catlike eyes with bags underneath them recites the specials in a bored voice, then slaps down their menus and walks away.

Mae leans in. "I think that was Heidi Tanner," she whispers. "Do you remember her from high school? She was so mean, and so pretty. I was in awe of her, but she terrified me."

"I wasn't really paying attention to her, back then or now," says Gabe. He had been staring at Mae in the candlelight, watching the way she pursed her lips and looked thoughtful and attentive as she listened to the specials, even though he knew she hated salmon and wasn't going to order it.

"Can you imagine living in this town forever?" She looks

away, down at the menu, sighs and flips the pages. "Steak for sure, why would you come here for anything else, right? And besides, I don't like salmon, so I won't get the special. What do you feel like? Want to share an appetizer?"

Gabe opens his menu, too. "Sure. Whatever you want."

They read their menus in silence until Heidi returns. She raises an overplucked eyebrow now, looks to Gabe, then to Mae. "Hey, I'm sorry to hear about your grandmother, Mae. But what are you still doing in town? I thought you were long gone, off marrying some rich guy in NYC and living happily ever after." Gabe can see Mae's cheeks reddening, even in the semidark. Now Heidi turns to him. "And you—never thought I'd see you back here at all, Gabe Broadbent. What rock have you been hiding under?"

Mae closes her menu with a snap. "We need a minute," she says. "Thanks." When Heidi is gone, Mae lowers her voice. "Do you want to leave?"

"It's fine. Don't worry about it." But he does. He longs for the anonymity of the city, where there are legions more people but you can have all the privacy you want. "It's just Heidi Tanner. She peaked in high school and now she works at a steak house. Who cares?"

"Okay. Right. Who cares? We're on our first official date. That's all that matters. Let's have fun. I want the filet mignon—stuffed, maybe? Do you think that would be good, or disgusting? And let's share a shrimp cocktail." She pushes her menu away.

"Sure, let's go for stuffed. A first." He closes his own menu and sips his water. "So, this guy you were going to marry—what was he like? There must have been some kind of redeeming quality, at least at first, before it all fell apart." He finds he feels jealous, even thinking of him. When Heidi mentioned her marrying the rich guy, he imagined Mae in

white silk, walking down a church aisle, eyes wide and ador-
ing. It made him feel sick, and now he's asked her about what
he knows is the last thing she wants to talk about.

But she only shakes her head. "I told you before. He wasn't
a good guy. He wasn't who I thought he was."

"And now, that's just it, it's over? Something went wrong,
you broke up and you're not in contact anymore?" He hates
the way he sounds, so possessive, but he's said it now.

She plays with her fork. "It was more than just something
going wrong."

"I'm sorry. I shouldn't have brought it up."

"It's fine." But she still doesn't look at him. "How about
you? What was your wife like? I can't picture you in a tux,
in a church, getting married…"

"Oh, we didn't do that. We got married at city hall and
had our reception at a dive bar."

Now she laughs. "Of course you did."

"It was her idea, actually."

There's a Don Henley song piping through the speakers
above, a song about memories and sunglasses. Gabe doesn't
want to talk about Natasha. The chair is uncomfortable. He
butters a piece of bread and takes a bite; it tastes funny, like
chemicals. "Natasha was… She was an anesthesiologist. You
have to go to school forever to be one of those, you have to
be completely focused. She was intense. One of those people who have it all together, knows exactly what she wants.
I never could figure out what she saw in me."

"Did you love her? Sorry, that's a stupid question. You
married her. Obviously you did."

"Did you love your guy?"

She doesn't answer. "Sorry," he says. "To answer your
question—well, I can't, actually. She told me I didn't love
her as much as I should have. I probably didn't. She told me

I was always in love with you. She's with someone else already. Pregnant, with twins. I think she's happy."

Awkward silence. "I think I'm bad at dates," Mae says.

"You're great. This is fine."

"It isn't, though, is it? This is awful. And I don't feel like stuffed steak. Let's get out of here. Grab a bottle of wine, go to the inn, order pizza. Come on." She stands and grabs his hand and they walk quickly out of the restaurant. When they're outside, he reaches for her and kisses her. He can taste it in his mouth—her toothpaste.

Dance in the rain.

Sometimes George drives in circles around the same town. Sometimes he drives straight through a town and vows never to return. He stays at the sort of motels he deplores. Lonely places, lost-soul havens. Then he drives to Vermont. He's always wanted to do that. He has ice cream, a lot of it. "What a world," he says to the girl who scoops his double cone. "You can have anything you want." She smiles at him in the way servers smile at old people.

He almost stays at a little inn he comes upon, an old white house with gables and black shutters, lights on in the windows welcoming him at dusk. But it would only make his broken heart worse, being somewhere nice like that without Lilly.

He finds the right government office in one of the towns he passes through; he applies to renew his long-expired passport; he stays at a Motel 6 while he waits for it to be ready. But he doesn't like it. He argued with the clerk the night before about their disingenuous slogan. "'We'll keep the lights on?' Don't you always have to keep the lights on? Don't some of these lights not turn off at all?" Although he supposes it can't really be called an argument, given how one-sided it was. The clerk gave him a look similar to the one the young

woman at the ice cream place had given him, but also dis-
missive, guarded.

During the night, he wakes, his body a tangle of aches and
pains. "Lilly!" he calls out. The dog growls, noses his arm.

He knows his destination, but drives off in the opposite
direction. There's a closer border but he's decided on the
Queenston–Lewiston Bridge, because he wants there to be a
substantial demarcation as he crosses into Canada, rather than
just an invisible divide that must be believed in and passed
over without really knowing when you did it. But he chose
the worst time: Friday morning. The lineup of trucks and
cars is five miles long. When he's about halfway to the front
of the line, Lilly comes back to him.

"George, don't do this. Don't go to them. They're not going
to be able to help you. They can't possibly have changed. You
should be protecting Mae from people like that, not trying
to bring them into her life."

He's so relieved, he can't speak at first, but then he gets
scared she might think he's ignoring her and disappear, so he
says, "I'm going and you don't have a say. You're gone, I'm
not enough and I'm sorry, but I'll never be certain of Gabe,
not completely, not after what happened. He's got a little of
Jonah in him, maybe always will."

She releases an irritated little sigh that's so welcome and
so familiar to him.

"Oh, Lilly," and he almost reaches for her. But he draws
back, for fear of reaching into nothingness.

"You're being absurd. You belong at the inn. You need
to go home."

"You actually still believe I belong at that inn, *his* inn?"

"Sixty-seven years spent in that one place, running it and
making it our own, and you still believe it isn't yours?"

"It's not mine and it never was, and now that you're gone I'm never going back."

The sun is pouring through the passenger side window and illuminating her. He has to focus on not plunging his foot down on the gas and rear-ending the SUV in front of him.

"Our lives were a lie," he says. "I can't go back there and face that truth. And I need to find a way to make sure she'll be all right, taken care of if I don't."

A sigh, like a breeze, in the car. The guard says, "Hello, sir. Your passport, please."

He looks at the dog. "Got immunization papers for him?"

"I've got his tags, on his collar."

The guard frowns. "Fine," he says, "but bring papers next time."

He hands George his passport, but George doesn't move. "Is that all?" George asks, hoping.

"Yeah. That's all. You're free to go."

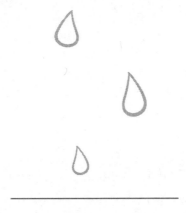

Stay in bed, sleep in.

Better yet if you have someone to stay in bed with.

(My mom said to cross that last part out, but I'm not

going to. This is an inn, what does she think the beds

are for?)

"We need a task." Mae is standing beside Gabe's bed when he opens his eyes. "We can't just wallow around the inn."

"We've been wallowing?"

"Well, no. But we haven't been doing much, just watching movies and ordering takeout. We might *start* wallowing if we're not careful. Let's go clean out the cabin. You're selling it, right? You have to clean it out first. I know it won't be easy, but I'll help you."

Gabe had actually been hoping the cabin, and the mess inside, would disappear. He hadn't even thought about selling it. Who would want it? And he'd been enjoying ordering takeout and watching movies with her. These past few days had been a pleasant blur. His only source of anxiety—working up the courage to do more than kiss her. He hasn't yet, but he's thought about almost nothing else.

"Come on, please?"

"You know I can't say no to you."

She's sitting on his cot, looking up at him. "I had this whole plan," she says, holding up the tape: The Smiths, *The Queen is Dead*. "Music and everything. I didn't really want to come out here and clean. It's actually pretty tidy in *here*—did your dad have a secret dusting habit, but in one room only?" She puts the tape down. "What I was really thinking was that we would come out here, and I would put on some Smiths, and I would..." She turns her head sideways, lowers her voice. "Well, to be honest, I'm trying to seduce you."

"Seduce me? Here?" He can't help it; he starts to laugh.

"The inn didn't feel right. Too full of ghosts. Oh, God, I'm so embarrassed."

"No. Don't be. Please." He takes the tape, looks at it, remembers that it used to be his, that he lent it to her and she never gave it back and he didn't care because he would have given her anything, even his favorite tape. He puts it in his old ghetto blaster, presses Play. Johnny Marr's guitar and Morrissey's voice fill the room. "You know, I actually *really* would like to be seduced by you—it's all I've been able to think about, trying to find a way to... But this is the worst place you could have picked. This place is full of ghosts, too." The music is taking him back in time. He loves her more because she is here with him in the present, but also because she is his past.

"I don't know what I was thinking. Forget it. This was stupid."

"Listen, it's not— My dad's ashes are in a coffee can in the kitchen. I brought them out here because I didn't know what to do with them. I can't really— It's not really conducive to— Oh, Christ. Sorry."

He steps toward the bed, leans down, kisses her. He wants her. Bad. And he's not going to give up this chance because of Jonah. "Stay here. I'll be back." He sees her face: doubt in her eyes. "I promise," he says, trying to smile and make her smile in return. "I'll be *right* back."

In the kitchen, he gets the coffee can. He puts on his jacket and boots and opens the door. There's a small pile of bricks on the side porch. He picks one up and opens the lid of the can. He puts the brick on top of the ashes and closes the lid.

He leaves the cabin and walks to the riverbank, steps off the island and walks several paces out. During the walk over with Mae, he saw a few of the flags for the ice holes the fisherman would have left early that morning. He hopes the holes haven't frozen over already. He finds one and looks down into it. He sees the slushy water a few feet below the surface, and he feels relieved. He thinks, *This is it, now you'll really be free.* He stands still for a moment, and then he drops the can into the hole and waits, fearing that it might float, even with the brick. It doesn't. It disappears. He imagines a muskie down there, snapping at the tin in confused rage as it sinks, chasing the irresistible metallic shine of the can all the way down to the bottom. He imagines the lid popping open and the ashes floating away with the currents, off in all directions.

He turns and walks back to the island. Outside the cabin he takes off his gloves and rubs snow over his hands to clean them.

Mae is still sitting on his bed. She says, "I thought about maybe being naked when you came in, you know, kind of Sharon Stone–ish because I remember you *loved* that scene. But…it's cold in here. And I'm not really Sharon Stone."

"You're way sexier than Sharon Stone, or anyone else."

She's lifting her shirt over her head now. She's not wearing a bra, she's wearing a lacy camisole instead and he can see her nipples through it, the pert shape of her small breasts. Her hair is down, cascading over her shoulders. How is it possible that this is happening, that he's this lucky? Even here, even in this place, he feels like the luckiest man in the world. And now she's in his arms. "Mae…"

He tries to be slow, he tries to be gentle—but she's not. She pulls him against her, bites his lower lip. He's nervous, self-conscious. It's so bright, what does she see? He's older now. Crow's-feet, stubble, is she still attracted to him? "I love you," she whispers. "I want you." He cups the back of her head, slides the camisole over her head, kisses her breasts, then her mouth again. He loves the way she smells. Her hair like fruit, like flowers, and her skin like coconut oil, like suntan lotion, like summers long past.

"What's that perfume?" he whispers.

"Dollar-store lotion…" He laughs into her hair, traverses her body with his lips and his hands. He loses himself, finds himself, but most importantly, finds her.

After, he traces her collarbone with his fingers, kisses her more gently. She turns and curves herself against his chest and he inhales the scent of her hair again. The music is still playing. Morrissey is now singing about the boy with the thorn in his side. That's not him anymore.

On the way home from the grocery store a few days later, Gabe sees an old red-and-white Chris-Craft at the end of a driveway with a for-sale sign taped to the windshield. He stops walking, puts down his bags, peeks inside. The interior was probably white once but is now yellowed and cracked. Gabe hears a cough behind him. A gray-haired man with a beard is watching him and smoking a pipe. He puffs out a cloud of smoke and says, "Still runs. Motor's still good. Just needs a little work on the interior. Nothing you can't handle. If you pay cash, you can take her home now."

"If she doesn't run, can I bring her back?"

"Sure, whatever." The man shrugs, smiles. "But I'm telling you, she does."

"I don't have anything to tow her with. Can you bring her to Summers' Inn for me, and I'll give you an extra fifty for the delivery?"

"No charge. You used to detail this boat for me at the marina when you were a kid, do you remember that?"

Gabe has to look more closely at the man. He remembers his face, and then, suddenly, this boat.

"It's good to see you back in town," the man says. "Happy to sell this boat to you. You always took such good care of her."

Gabe smiles to himself as he walks home, to the inn. People remember him as more than what he had thought of himself for so many years. He isn't just Jonah Broadbent's useless, abused son. He left the good parts of himself here, too, not just the bad. And now he's back to claim them. He can't wait to tell Mae about the boat.

Life doesn't stop just because you're on vacation.

Make a to-do list you can tackle when you get home.

M ae pads down the hall in her moccasin slippers; she slept late. She can hear Gabe typing in the kitchen. He's working on a freelance project, as he does most mornings now. It's for a magazine: graphics to go with the stories. Mae hovered around him for the first few days and it discomfited her, this aimlessness and dependence, so strong in part because of how worried she is about the whereabouts of her grandfather—and how frustrated she is that he's taken to leaving messages on the sly, using his password to the call answering service so he can inform them that he is fine, just driving around, they shouldn't worry—and no other details, no way to reach him, no way to tell him she's sorry, or ask him to come home, tell him that three weeks are enough, *enough now*, that she needs him back.

She's been unsettled by something else, too, by the way it feels the roles between her and Gabe have reversed. He takes care of her now. And what does she have to offer him, aside from memories of a young girl he fell in love with?

To distract herself from all this, she has created for herself the task of going through boxes upstairs in the attic, sorting her grandmother's things. "It's been almost a month since the funeral," she said to Gabe. "These things need to be done."

It's pointless, though: Lilly kept everything organized and George had been in the navy and took pride in always keeping everything "shipshape." You have to be systematic when you live in an inn, Lilly would say. Clutter could never be in view—and couldn't be out of view either, waiting to tumble out and take over at the end of the season. Every box Mae has opened has been filled with exactly what it said it would contain, in Lilly's bold, boxy letters. "Invoices."

"Mae/School."

"Extra napkins."

She kisses Gabe good morning and pours herself a coffee. There's a podcast on; he likes to listen to them while he works. She brings the milk to the table and sits, tries to listen, too, even though she's come in in the middle and feels lost.

"The river is starting to thaw already," she observes. "Early this year."

"Yeah," he says. "I've noticed. Maybe when it's thawed completely we can get out on the boat."

"The boat. Maybe." Every time he mentions it, she feels a wave of nausea. Now that she's lost so many people to it, she can hardly look at the river.

"Any plans for today?"

She has stirred the milk into her coffee and is putting it back in the fridge. Her face is suddenly hot and she stays in front of the open fridge door for a moment before replacing the milk and turning back to him. "Lots of plans. I should get back to the attic. There's so much to do. Good luck with your project, honey." She winces as she heads for the swinging kitchen door. *Honey?* It doesn't feel natural to call him that. Domestic bliss doesn't seem to suit her anymore, not since that last night in New York, when she had reveled in it, been so sure of it, been so sure of a person she didn't actually know. Now she just keeps waiting for someone to pull the rug out.

Back in the attic, the dust makes her sneeze, but still she keeps digging. She's found a box of memorabilia from when her mother was a baby: a tiny sleeper, a porcelain box labeled "Teeth" that she decides not to open, a baptismal candle, report cards, school photos. But not what she's looking for: none of Virginia's old journals, if she ever kept any; no letters between her and Mae's father, and there must have been those. Mae knows her parents' relationship wasn't perfect. In fact, it was disastrous in the end. But Virginia and Chase had loved each other. No matter what else had happened, it had been true love. Hadn't it?

"Not even a wedding photo?" she says aloud, exasperated. But then she realizes, with a sinking sensation in the pit of her stomach, that this is her own fault. Lilly gave Mae the small wedding album years ago—and Mae left it at Peter's apartment with all her other things. It's probably in a New York garbage dump now.

She stands and wipes her dusty hands on her knees, leaves open boxes and scattered contents behind when she goes back downstairs. Gabe is on the phone when she peeks her head into the kitchen. "I'm going to Viv's," she mouths, and he nods, blows her a kiss.

There's warmth in the breeze and Mae can feel the melted river water in it, the promise of spring. She looks toward the boathouse and imagines being out on the river with Gabe. Water droplets spraying her arms, wind in her air, sun in her eyes. And there's a child in this unbidden reverie, a child in the boat with them, with messy hair and an orange life jacket and a smile that's somehow familiar. Mae starts to walk faster.

"Do you want tea today?" Viv asks her when she's inside her kitchen.

Mae shakes her head. "I have a question," she says as Viv fills the kettle anyway.

"Why didn't my grandmother save any of my mother's things?"

Vivian is fussing with the teapot. "Your mother wasn't the sentimental type. Neither was your grandmother. Maybe there just wasn't anything to save."

"But there had to have been—letters from when my dad was back home with his family after they met, before he ran away to be with her. He was home without her for months. They must have written to each other."

"They must have, you're right."

Mae is frustrated. Viv knows everything, she was Lilly's confidant. And Mae is on the outside, even now. "Do you think she would have actually thrown my mother's things away, her letters, her pictures?"

Viv pours hot water into the kettle. "That's possible."

"Why?"

"Because maybe it hurt her to see them. People do things like that. I threw out my first wedding album before I knew better."

Peter, suddenly, his face in her mind. Mae doesn't have photo albums, but there's a phone full of pictures, ready to drag her back into the past if she ever turns it on again. She has contemplated throwing it into the river, the one place she knows you can truly lose something in, forever. "It's hard not to want to."

"I know. But eventually, you have to focus on the future. You seem to have one, with Gabe."

Mae smiles; it's involuntary. The sound of his name does it every time, even with all her fears. And Viv is the only person she talks to these days, other than Gabe—the only person she can talk about Gabe *to*. "He bought a boat," she says. "That means, I think, that he wants to stay for a while. Maybe forever."

"Boats aren't forever."

"I know that. I just— I think he was trying to tell me that, by buying it, but in truth it just upset me. I don't ever want to go in a boat, or out on the river, again."

"You might not feel that way forever."

"But I might."

"And he should be able to read your mind?"

She smiles again. "Yeah. He should."

Viv smiles, too. "Do you want to stay? Forever, or at least for a while?"

This line of questioning is making her nervous. It reminds Mac of the way she would feel at the police station. Backed into a corner, unsure of the truth. But this is Viv, who doesn't want anything from her, who doesn't have an ulterior motive. "I don't know," she answers, over the sound in her ears of her rapidly beating heart. "He's started working again on his freelance stuff. He can do it from anywhere, says he'll only have to go to the city once in a while for meetings. And being here indefinitely seems to be the subtext. I heard him on the phone a few days ago giving up his apartment."

"That certainly does seem like something. But…you have reservations. It makes you nervous."

"I don't know what to do with myself. Even the boat, even if I get over it—I have no money to contribute to fixing it up, but he seems to want it to be something we share. It's embarrassing. He keeps calling it 'ours' but it's not, it's his. And if we stay here together, what do I do, get a job at the Dollar Barn? I have an MBA. It feels like we're playing house, pretending, and eventually reality is going to set in and it's all going to be over." She's afraid of the truth, she realizes, afraid that saying all this aloud will somehow seal her fate.

"Start a business, then. You have an MBA, you just said it. Do something with it."

"It's not that easy."

"Isn't it? Seems to me you're sitting on a business right now, one that—with a bit of work, granted, but still—could be up and running again in no time. Tourism is booming. And you've got a prime spot."

"I've got nothing. It's not mine, and who knows what Grandpa wants to do with it? Plus, the place is falling apart. Those repairs would take money and—" she looks up at Viv and wonders if Lilly got the chance to tell her friend about the mess with Peter, about the lost money, before she died. She lets the sentence trail off.

"This might not be what you want to hear," Viv says. "But it doesn't matter what George wants. He's at the end of his life. Easy now, don't look so shocked, I'm not saying he's going to die imminently, but he's not going to be starting down any new paths or helping to breathe new life into that old inn when he gets back here. It's you who's going to have to be taking care of him, and if doing something like starting up the business again is going to give you the means to do that, then why not? Find a way."

"It's a risk."

"Are you sure about that? A heritage inn with plenty of space in an established tourist town doesn't seem like a risk at all."

"I don't know the first thing about running an inn."

"You could learn."

"Maybe I don't *want* to run an inn."

"Fine, then, don't. Get your grandfather's permission to sell the place, and do something else with the money, something that makes more sense for you."

"I can't just sell it out from under him."

"He can't stay away forever. Look, you've had a bad run, a bad relationship. And, all right, at the moment you don't

have a lot going for you. Which is why it's especially important for you to start thinking about your own best interests,
instead of other people's."

"You sound like a therapist."

"Therapist, actress. They're very similar."

Mae laughs. "How so?"

But Viv's expression is serious. "In order to act like another person, you have to observe them until you know, really know, what it might feel like to be them."

From Viv's kitchen window, Mae has a direct view of Island 51, just like at home. "Does this apply to anyone?" she
asks, gazing out at the broken-down shack. "Even someone
like Jonah Broadbent? Would you ever want to imagine what
it might be like to be someone like that?" She's been thinking of Jonah more and more as she gets closer and closer to
Gabe and bears witness to the scars that he still lives with,
scars inflicted by his father. In bed one morning, while he
was still asleep, she saw another cigarette burn on his back,
faint but still there, one he must have hidden from her when
they were kids, and she couldn't stop her silent tears.

"Especially someone like him. Jonah's father was a mon-
ster. Micah. These biblical names." She pauses. "And Gabriel,
the angel. I wonder if his mother did that on purpose. Maybe
he was supposed to save them."

"Did you know her?"

Viv shakes her head. "No. She wasn't around too long, and
kept to herself, out on that island with Jonah until she was
gone one day. But I did know Jonah's mother, somewhat. I
know that Jonah's father almost killed her once. Concussed
her so badly she was never the same. Everyone knew she
hadn't really fallen down the stairs, but no one did anything
because you didn't back then, in this town. I regret it. I think
a lot of people do, but what does it matter?" Viv shakes her

head. "I'm so glad your grandparents finally stepped in when it came to Gabe, to stop that cycle of hurt people hurting other people. I've seen it happen too many times."

Hurt people hurting other people. Now Mae's fears are tight on her heels, when she had come here to get away from them. She keeps her eyes on the shack, finds herself wishing it didn't exist, that Gabe had been given the childhood he deserved.

"Gabe is a good man," Viv says, as if she can read Mae's thoughts.

"I'm afraid something is going to go wrong." She closes her eyes, and the shack is gone, finally.

"Something might. But you need to focus on other things, rather than how scared you are."

She tries to do that. She tries not to be afraid. "I really messed things up back in New York." She opens her eyes again, lets herself breathe. "I made so many mistakes." It feels good, now that her heart rate is returning to normal, to talk to Viv this way. Familiar in a way Mae can't put her finger on.

"And I've made a lot of mistakes in my life. If I let fear of failure stop me, I'd never have accomplished anything. I'd have stayed in this town forever. Now, come on, Mae, go back home, stop scrabbling through the past. There's a man over there who adores you. Also, let him worry about the boat. Men like to have their little projects. And you're going to be fine."

A mist has formed over the river, and as Mae walks home, she can't see anything out there. Island 51 is completely obscured, like it never existed.

She goes straight upstairs to the attic. She opens a box that says "Mae/High School." Inside the cover of an eleventh-grade science notebook, her girlish script reads *Mr. and Mrs. Gabriel Broadbent. Mae Summers-Broadbent. Mae Summers, wife of Gabe Broadbent.* That last one had been her favorite, she remembers. She traces the handwriting with a fingernail now. Then she hears footsteps on the stairs and flips the notebook shut. *"Stop scrabbling through the past." This is the present.*

Gabe is standing in the low doorway. "You're only up here, and I'm in the kitchen. I miss you. Is that idiotic?"

"Yes," she says. "Completely. Come here."

Visit the Fitzgerald & Lee boat shop, where magnificent boats have been crafted since 1930—and my grandfather, Angus (Lilly's dad), worked as a boatbuilder.

Look for his picture in the archives.

G abe is alone on Island 51. He's been out here every day or so for the past week, first to finish cleaning his father's things out of the cabin, and then to rake the grounds. He knows he could easily sell the island and be rid of it, that the islands around here rarely go up for sale, and when they do there's a bidding war. But every time he thinks about selling, he also starts to consider the other things he could do with the island. Tear down the cabin and build himself a little office, perhaps, a log shack where he could work every day. He imagines a fireplace there in winter, sees himself crossing the ice with his laptop. He'd be out of Mae's way then, because she can't possibly want him around all the time, can she?

But then he wonders if it's selfish, doing something here that's just for himself. He'd seen a flash of hurt in Mae's eyes when he came home and said he'd bought the boat, and it had occurred to him then that he needed to work on being a partner, on making decisions that included her, too. That maybe the river was still a sensitive topic for her. When he'd tried to apologize, she'd waved him off.

He rakes one side of the shoreline and moves to the other. He could build a cabin they could spend summer weekends in. Maybe something unique, a modern tree house, a shipping container structure. He can picture Mae on the newly immaculate shore, dipping her toes into the water, swimming out and beckoning him to join. Maybe he'll go home and talk to her about this. He wants to make plans that will mean that he's staying, that will mean she wants him to, that prove they have a future.

One last pass of the rake, and he hits an obstruction. He digs in harder, and a fish bone rib cage is revealed. He bends down and starts brushing away the wet dirt with his hands. As he reveals more of the skeleton, he sees how huge this fish was. Once he gets to the head, Gabe knows it's a muskie: there's the wide beaklike mouth, the big jaw and jagged teeth, still intact. No wonder he was so afraid of these fish as a child.

The skeleton is about five feet long, and wide, too, maybe two feet in diameter. Gabe knows the muskie record in the bay is just over four feet, sixty pounds. Virginia caught it. Her name is on the list on the side of the town hall, right at the top, a rare female name among all the male anglers, and the most accomplished of all of them. Sometimes when they were kids, Gabe and Mae would walk into town and stand in front of that list. "I just need to make sure," Mae would say. "I just need to make sure she existed."

Gabe peers inside the giant jaws, and inside is his father's signature lure. Jonah whittled his lures from birch branches, then added red paint, little flashes of metal. Gabe's father definitely caught this fish. But he didn't tell anyone. It makes Gabe think of how he didn't tell George the truth about the money, even though he could feel it hanging between them, George's cautious acceptance tempered by mistrust, before he took off on them. "Why not tell him next time he calls?" Mae had asked him one night. "You're not a thief, and he should know that. Maybe he'll come back if he does."

"But she doesn't deserve that, Lilly doesn't. You know I'm

right. She's not here to defend herself, and just because I am doesn't mean I should."

She had told him she loved him then, and she had cried, and he had known that there were too many things he was never going to be able to say to her.

A cold wind comes out of nowhere and cuffs Gabe in the side of the face, a remnant of winter, straight from the north. Gabe leaves the rake lying in the sand. He gets in his boat and heads for shore. Mae is sitting on the end of the dock. She smiles and waves. He's not going to talk to her about building anything together on this island, he decides. He's going to list it and sell it because the specter of Jonah still lives there, no matter that Gabe tossed his ashes into the river. *Your mom wasn't the best angler in the bay after all.* He can't say this to her, but he can imagine it and he hates that. *And George, he isn't really your grandfather. And what Lilly did, it still hurts me, even though I pretend it doesn't. You can't imagine how badly I wish she were still here, too, so I could tell her that. So I could prove to her that I'm enough for you and then maybe truly believe it myself.*

"Let's go to the real estate office," he says. "I need to get rid of that place for good."

Mae looks up at him, tilts her head, and for a moment he thinks she's going to ask him what happened out there. But all she says is "Of course. If that's what you want, let's go."

*V*irginia *turns toward the opening of the river. There's a dark
shape up ahead, a gaping hole in the ice and a boat, their
hovercraft, upside down. She cries out, "No!" In her mind, over
and over, she thinks,* Oh, God, please don't let him be gone.
I'll stand by him and get him through this. I'll pay more attention. I won't fight with him. We'll get him through this.

*She runs through the rain. She calls his name, but the wind car-
ries away her voice. As she gets closer, she realizes the problem. How
will she do this? How exactly will she get close enough to the hole
and the flipped hovercraft without falling in? How will she move the
craft and what will she find when she does?*

*Then she sees it: an arm, a hand—his—reaching out from under
the boat. Or maybe not reaching. Maybe just floating. But she tells
herself,* It's not too late. Never too late. *When she's a few feet
away, she starts to crawl. She gets close enough to grab the hand
and she pulls as hard as she can, but he's stuck under the hovercraft.*
"Hold on. Just hold on."

*The ice around her is starting to crack. She slides her legs into the
water. She pushes the hovercraft and it moves, a little at first and
then a lot. She sees tools spilled out of a toolbox, onto the ice, and
all at once realizes he went out in the craft without her because he
was going to their island to work on the cabin.* "Oh, Chase..." *His*

hand and arm and then the rest of his body come free of the craft. But when her husband's face is in view it's not the face she knows. It's all wrong. Not the right color, and his eyes are open, unblinking, staring at nothing.

The ice gives way and she's falling into the river. The water is cold and then suddenly hot. She reaches for Chase, wraps one arm around him and grasps for the edge of the hole. She tries to pull him up, but instead, they're sinking.

How is it that she sees Mae's face? She knows Mae is not here. But if she doesn't save Chase, save herself, then what of Mae? She strains for the surface, makes it over the lip of the ice and pulls them both up and over, somehow. "Chase," she whispers through lips swollen with cold. She lays her body over him, puts her head against his chest, waits to hear a heartbeat. But there's only silence. She's failed.

The rain is slowing down. Someone will come. If only Virginia can stay awake.

And then she sees him: an apparition, Jonah in his cutter, coming toward her.

Soon, he's there, by her side. "I'm so sorry," he says.

"It's okay, it's all right. Don't cry, Jonah." She would have forgiven anyone anything, just to have Chase back, just to be with Mae again, but she does mean it when she says, "You didn't do anything wrong, it's all right, it's okay." Then she closes her eyes and succumbs to the darkness. He holds on to her for a moment, and he cries, but she's too far gone to hear his sobs. Then he lifts her carefully, and carries her to his cutter. He returns, lifts Chase and brings him there, too.

PART THREE

Go see a movie at the Bay Drive-in Theatre.

"I have a story for you," Lilly says after a few miles. This has become her habit: appearing to him while he's driving and telling her stories. "There was a dance, at the high school, in the gym. For the end of the year. Viv was on the committee, it was a ragtime theme, do you remember? I was sixteen and you were eighteen."

George has heard this one before, of course. "I don't remember any of the dances. Too painful. I couldn't dance to save my life. I'd stand in a corner and wait for it to be over."

"I walked up to you while you were getting yourself some punch, thinking I might ask you to dance. But I lost my nerve, because I saw it in your eyes—your eyes, I had just noticed, were very nice and very blue."

"Saw what in my eyes?"

"That when you looked at me you saw a pal. Tommy's little sister, Viv's friend, just plain old Lilly with her dishpan hair and muddy green eyes."

He can see the moment clearly now. She's wrong about her eyes not being beautiful. Her eyes were the color of the river in spring and that was the moment he noticed it. "I wanted to dance with you, but I didn't know the bloody one-step and the cakewalk and whatever it was. Everett knew all those. You should have danced with him."

"I did," she says. "But there was a slow song, and it was you I wanted to dance with to that one." She starts to sing, Irving Berlin. "'How much do I love you? / I'll tell you no lie. / How deep is the ocean? / How high is the sky?...'?" She laughs like a young girl, the one he remembers. His car hurtles down the highway, through time and blue sky, and for just a moment, he feels good. "I loved you," she says. "I always have. It just took you a while to catch up."

He's about to tell her he's always loved her, too. But when he looks over, she's gone again. Then there are lights blinking in his rearview mirror. A police car. And the lights are for him.

George was upset about his first ever speeding ticket initially, but then he propped it on his dash like a badge of honor. "Rebel without a cause, that's me," he says, but Lilly still isn't back. There's no one but the dog to talk to. He's not going to pay this ticket. Once he's done with this trip, it's not going to matter if they take his license away. Once he's done with this trip, he'll be done with everything.

He decides to delay his final destination a little more, to drive to Niagara Falls, just for the hell of it, and goes all the way back the way he came, almost to the border again. He likes it there a little. He stays for almost a week, at a pet-friendly dump of a hotel at the edge of the tourist area, with its garish haunted houses and Ripley's Believe It or Not! museums. He goes for walks, he goes to a wax museum, he stands and looks out at the falls and remembers his and Lilly's short honeymoon, over on the American side. He misses her. There are moments when he believes her, believes that maybe she really did love him. There are moments he feels like a regular person. But those moments are fleeting.

Eventually, he gets back in the car, fills up the gas tank, consults his map, starts driving again. He can't avoid it any longer. He has a task. He likes the name of the road he's on: Queen Elizabeth Way. And about a mile in, there's Lilly, at his side again. He turns the talk-radio station down.

"You never ran away from anything before," she says.

"I never could. I always had to stay. How could I have run away from you and our obligations?"

"Did you ever want to run the inn?"

Silence. And then, because there's no point in lying to her, he says, "No. Actually, I would have loved to be a rancher. Did you ever know that? I used to have a dream about getting out of the bay, away from the river, going somewhere completely different, maybe west, with mountains and wide-open space and just— I used to imagine you and me and the little family we would have, out somewhere in the middle of nowhere, just us and the sky. I didn't tell Everett that on the ship, but that's what I dreamed of most of the time. You, and the stars. Our stars."

"You could have told me. We could have said no to Everett's parents."

"How could I? When Everett's family wanted to give me the inn, how could I have said no? And I thought it was what *you* wanted, to live there, to raise his child there, because that was the right thing to do to honor him." He realizes what he has said. *Raise his child.*

"You always knew the truth."

The truth. Did he? Did he know everything? And who else knew? "Did Vivian know about Virginia?" His tone has an abrupt edge. He is able to grasp at the edges of his anger again. For Vivian to know, to officially know, and for him not to, for him to be the one who had to pretend, that would be a betrayal of a different kind.

She doesn't answer.

"Lillian?" he presses.

"Don't, George. Don't. She was yours in all the ways that matter. I saw it from the day Virginia was born. I felt it, and you did, too. Don't say you didn't."

Morning light shining in the window of the hospital room and illuminating Virginia's red-gold peach fuzz just so. And a love so strong he had to sit down. Yes, he remembers. It rendered him helpless and intensely grateful all at the same time. Sitting there, his head fogged up with the mystery of childbirth—when moments before he had been surrounded by nurses, had been trying not to look at the blood on the floor, had felt like a fish out of water—suddenly he could feel Everett there beside him, offering his approval. *Guardian. Father.* For once, George hadn't felt like a second choice.

George thinks he needs to turn on the windshield wipers, that it has unexpectedly started to rain. But it's not rain at all: he's crying, tears so thick he has to veer off the highway, pull the car over to the shoulder of the road. He wishes he could reach out and bury his face in Lilly's neck. But he has nothing to reach for.

Alexandria Bay has the best flea market.
You never know what surprises you'll find.

The phone rings while Mae is in the pantry looking for stewed tomatoes; Gabe answers it. "It's a Detective Lamoglea," he says, concern in his eyes.

She takes the phone, listens while Lamoglea tells her that Peter has been apprehended in South Africa and is in the process of being extradited back to the United States. This can't be her life he's talking about, this can't be something or someone she was ever involved with. When he had called that night, had he been looking for help? Had he actually thought she might help him hide, or something crazy like that? She looks down at the can of tomatoes in her hands and can't remember what she wanted with them.

"Do you need anything from me?" is all she says, glancing at Gabe, trying to keep her tone level.

"Not for now. A trial will take a while. I don't expect to be back in touch any time soon. I just thought you should know, before you read it in the news."

After she hangs up, she tells Gabe her apartment was broken in to back in the city. She's amazed at how easily the lie pours out. "We should be honest with each other about everything," she has told him during the nights when they stay awake, pouring their hearts into each other's as the moonlight pours across their bed. But it applies only to him, apparently. This is a cave she's rolling a boulder in front of. These are things he can never know. "The police had a lead on the break-in, that's why they called." He seems to believe her. As she heats the tomatoes, he tells her a story about his first apartment being broken in to, about how the intruders trashed the place when they couldn't find anything good to take. He laughs a little—"Who would want six hoodies and a bunch of Philip Roth novels, right?"—and the moment passes.

Mae can't sleep that night. She lies awake beside Gabe until the morning light grows strong enough to put to rest any idea of sleeping. Her nausea grows along with the light. It never went away after Lilly died, but it's been getting worse. It must be the anxiety she feels about Detective Lamoglea's call. Or she ate something that didn't agree with her. That's all it is.

She's forced from the bed and into the bathroom, and she barely makes it. After, she rinses out her mouth and stares at her pale face in the mirror. *Don't panic.* But as she turns on the shower, she tries to remember the last time she had her period. She can't. She imagines a tiny swell when she places her hand low on her belly.

Is it possible to just know something like this about herself, to just know, suddenly, that what she suspects is true? If it is, it will be the first time she's known herself at all.

"Mae, please, what's going on? Are you sick? Come out. Talk to me."

She's sitting on the bath mat on the bathroom floor upstairs, with her back against the tub and her head against the door. She has the test stick in her hand. She thinks about sliding it under the door, but it won't fit and anyway, that isn't the best way to tell him this kind of news. But what is the best way? How do you tell something like this to someone you've been with for only a month? How do you tell him you're pregnant with another man's baby, that it can't possibly be his baby, that instead the father is a man who is a felon, soon to be convicted?

He knocks again. "Mae!"

She unlocks the door. He enters, stares at her sitting on the floor.

She holds up the test.

"There were two in the box. I did them both. Both positive."

He takes the test from her.

"Yikes. A baby," he says. Mae reads his expression easily. It's like he's an animal caught in headlights, an animal about to turn and run away into the forest.

But he doesn't run. He lowers down to the floor and sits beside her with his back against the tub. He reaches for her clammy hand.

She says, "I'm about two months pregnant, I think."

His expression doesn't change.

"I've been feeling sick for a long time. And we didn't... It hasn't been long enough." A slow dawning on his face; she's nostalgic for every moment that came before this one—all gone now.

"So that means...?" He's staring over her shoulder now. Will he ever look her in the eye again?

"The baby is Peter's. My ex-fiancé's. He's the father."

He pulls his hand away. "Are you going to tell him?"

"I don't have any way to reach him. And I don't want him in my life."

"Are you going to keep...it?"

Her heart sinks past the rock bottom she believed she had already reached. "It?" she repeats.

"Well, you don't know if it's—sorry—if it's a boy or girl."

"Stop. Just stop saying 'it.'"

He goes silent on her. He's waiting for an answer to the question. "I'm still the mother. You realize that, don't you?" she says. "But because you're not the father, you think I shouldn't keep the baby?" She hates the way her voice sounds in her ears. She hates how angry she is at him, and how bewildered he is, how distant now. She hates that what she wants so much involves sacrificing the person she needs most.

"That's not what I meant. I just wanted to—"

"Never mind," she says. "The answer is yes. I want a baby. This baby. Despite the circumstances." Her eyes fill with tears. "For a few minutes, before I realized, when I thought it was ours, I felt so happy. Even though I was scared. And when I did realize— I'm sorry. But it didn't change the way I felt. I guess this means I'm losing you."

"You're not losing me."

"No?"

There's too much silence, but then it's over. "No. This is a lot to take in. But I'm still here."

"You don't have to—"

"I know I don't have to. But I want to. Nothing has to change, okay? I've never thought about having kids, but that's only because there's never been anyone I wanted to have kids with. It's still us. We can do this."

She manages to take a breath, letting his words reach her, yet again, reaching for that lifeline, as she always does with him. Will there be a last time? He moves closer. He's there. He is. He's holding her hand again. She leans in close; she needs to see his eyes. "I love you," he continues. "I'm not going anywhere."

I love you, too, she wants to say, but nothing comes out. She can only squeeze his hand, hard.

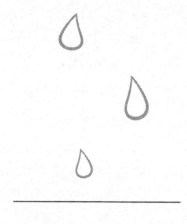

Is it Sunday?

Buy the New York Times and read it from cover to cover.

A man a few chairs down in the waiting room was reading a newspaper but is now incessantly cracking his knuckles. Gabe tries to ignore him but this becomes impossible when the man speaks to him. "Nervous habit. And it's our third—you'd think I'd be used to it by now."

Gabe smiles and nods.

"Is it your first? Seems like it. You look really nervous."

"Uh. Yeah."

"Well, I won't scare you, then. The wife'll never try to punch you out while she's in labor. And changing diapers? Just great, man, totally fun." Gabe looks away.

Just then the nurse comes into the room and says, "Partner of Amanda Edwards?" and the man jumps up, spilling the newspaper pages to the floor.

"That's me! Good luck, man."

"Yeah—thanks. You, too."

Gabe leans over and picks up the pages of the paper on the floor. He scans the headlines, but can't focus. Mae seems to have been in there a long time. But what does he know about how long is too long? If something is wrong, will they come out and get him? What if something is going to happen to her, what if this baby is going to hurt her in some way? It makes his hands sweat and his eyes water, this idea. And there's resentment, too. This baby. He's stopped calling the baby "it"—but he can't start calling it "his."

He's relieved when he looks up and sees Mae hovering in the door frame at the front of the waiting room.

But then he remembers this wasn't how it was supposed to go. He jumps up, and the newspaper is on the floor again. "Are you okay?" he says when he gets closer to her. "Is the baby okay? What happened?"

"It's just— I'm fine. We're fine. I think the radiologist didn't know you were supposed to come in. Maybe because I didn't have you as my partner in my intake file. Sorry. Next time?"

"Oh. Sure. Yeah. Next time." His gut churns. There's more to it. She won't look at him. And he knows what it means: she didn't want him in there. She didn't want to share the experience with him. If she can't accept him as the father, how will he be able to?

He helps her into her coat and they leave. They wait for the bus to take them to Alexandria Bay from Watertown. It starts to rain and he pulls her into the shelter. He can't stop doing these things for her now; he wants to protect her, and the baby.

Or maybe he wants to protect her *from* the baby. This baby who isn't his, and never will be his.

"What was it like?" he asks. "Seeing...the baby?" *I wanted to be there. That was the moment the baby was supposed to become mine, too. Why didn't you let me?*

Her eyes light up. "I heard the heartbeat. And he—or she—was sucking a thumb."

He forces a smile. He can do this, because he would do anything for her. He loves her. "We didn't talk about that part," he says. "Do you want to find out the sex? It doesn't matter to me, truly. Whatever you want."

She looks away from him. "There's the bus" is all she says.

I know I'm always suggesting getting in the car and getting out of here when it's raining; maybe it's because I've hardly ever left this town myself.
But driving in the rain can be a nice way to pass the time.
Go to Canton, a few towns over, for some great pizza if you need a destination.

George is on an underpass, stuck in afternoon traffic, on a street called Spadina. He turns right and crawls along. A streetcar clangs past, red, white and black. Cars honk. A man wanders the rows of cars with a coffee cup and a sign that says Down on My Luck. George opens his window and hands the man a twenty, which is the smallest bill he has, and the man says, "Thank you, sir. Thank you, sir," over and over, until George closes the window because he doesn't know what else to do.

"Don't do this, George," Lilly says once the window is closed.

"I told you, I have to. You know I do. Will you leave me for good if I do?"

Traffic is stopped again; he looks over at her. Her eyes are sad and she seems less substantial than usual. "I'm already gone, George," she says. "You know that."

"Because of me." His voice cracks like a dish dropped on the floor. "Because of me, you're dead, you're gone. And that's why I can't be her one and only official living family member. I'm not to be trusted. That's why I have to do this. To make amends. Give something back to Mae."

Bud scrambles to attention because George has raised his

voice. He puts his head on George's shoulder. George shrugs him off.

"You know that when Virginia set her mind to something, there was never going to be any stopping her," Lilly says. "If you're thinking it's your fault she died, it's mine, too."

"No. It's the father's job, the man's job, to lay down the law."

Lilly laughs, surprising him. "You were never the sort of man to 'lay down the law,' George."

"You're ridiculing me."

"I'm not. I love you for it. You're kind, gentle, accepting. If we had tried to bend a child like Virginia to our will, we would have lost her long before."

"If Everett had lived, everything would have been different."

"Of course it would have. But I was happy I got to spend my life with you, George. That's the truth."

It always ends and begins in the truth.

George feels confused. Confused by her words, by the traffic, by the unfamiliar street names. "I need to find my way," he says. He stops the car at a gas station with a phone booth. But before he gets out, he faces Lilly. "Don't go," he says. "Please just stay with me while I do this. Don't leave me." She doesn't answer.

He goes inside the gas station and gets five dollars in change, asks for it in quarters, fills his pocket with change. "I would have felt rich with all these quarters when I was a little boy," he says to the man behind the counter. But the blank look on the man's face makes him wish he hadn't spoken. He's always experiencing this now when he's out in the world. He doesn't translate as a person in general. He is a relic. Everything moves so fast, and it's passed him by. He jingles the quarters. He buys some breath mints and some terrible coffee.

It's cold inside the phone booth. Cold people, that was what Lilly had always called the Rutherfords, Chase's parents. They proved that, irrevocably, when they came to take their son's body home and refused to see Mae. George and Lilly had been too broken to fight a battle they would probably lose to people with money and power they didn't have. And, George remembers, in his paralyzing grief, he had blamed Chase for what happened. He had wanted him gone, no matter the pain it might cause Mae, whose father would become nothing but a black hole—a black hole shaped like all the things Chase could have been but never was.

George expects he'll have to call all the *D* or *A* Rutherfords in the phone book, but he gets Delia on his second try.

"Yes?"

He is silent. Frozen. *Cold people.*

"Who's there? Who is this?"

"Delia?"

"Yes?" she repeats, irritation creeping in. "Who is calling?"

"George Summers."

"What is it that you want?"

"I'm in Toronto," he says. "I came to see you and Anthony."

"Why would you do such a thing?"

"Because I'd like to talk to you." Silence. "Lilly has died," he adds, and this feels disloyal. He can see her, sitting there in the car. He's relieved she's still there. She waves at him and he waves back.

"Where are you, exactly?"

"Downtown. Spadina and…Front Street, I think. I can see the CN Tower."

"You can see that vulgar phallus of a tower from most places in Toronto. Anyway, I'm in the north end, nowhere close to where you are. The Bridle Path. Eleven Hill Point Road." She hangs up without saying goodbye.

"Eleven Hill Point Road," he repeats to Lilly when he gets in the car.

"Oh, George."

He finds the street on his map, then drives back the way he came and out onto a highway that curves around the city. Lilly is silent, staring out the window at the pitiful brown river that has appeared beside them.

He drives through a vast treed valley and under bridges. When he's in Delia's neighborhood there are no more tall buildings, just houses larger than most of the houses George has ever seen in his life, with huge columns at the front, or sweeping balconies on all sides, or multiple gables with peaked, church-like windows. There are tennis courts, swimming pools, multicar garages. Delia's house has all three of these things, and a fountain in the driveway that's filled with leaves.

"Okay, then," he says to Lilly. She reaches out her hand toward him, but he draws back just as they are about to touch. He gets out of the car.

Bud is hesitating at the bottom of the stone staircase. "Come on, boy. Nothing to be afraid of." He wishes he could believe this himself.

Man and dog approach the door together: it's large, wide, glossy black. No bell that he can see, just a knocker in the shape of an angry lion's head. George doesn't want to touch it but he must. He lifts his hand, he knocks. Enough time passes that he thinks perhaps she won't answer, but then the door swings open. Delia is swathed in a tawny-colored fur coat and is wearing large diamond earrings that pull her earlobes down in a manner that George finds obscene to look at. Her hair is still auburn, but there is white showing at the crown.

"Hello, Delia. Thank you for allowing me to stop by at such short notice." He has the urge to bow, to laugh stupidly. Bud sits back on his haunches.

"Hello, George." Her skin is like crepe paper. The rouge on her cheeks is not quite rubbed in. "You didn't mention a dog."

"All right with you if he comes in?"

"Not really, but if you leave him running around the yard I'll be stepping in his shit for weeks."

Inside, he gives her his coat when she offers to take it; she hangs it unceremoniously over the banister. As soon as his coat is off he realizes the house is freezing. He wonders if she has fallen on hard times and can't afford to heat the house, or if the heat is broken, or if she's just cheap. Maybe she turned it off when he said he was coming, so he wouldn't stay long.

"Why have you come?"

"Lilly is dead."

"You said that on the telephone. I'm not sure that merits traveling here to tell me in person. I didn't call you when Anthony died."

He clears his throat. "Oh. I didn't know your husband had died. Well, I'm sorry. But... Mae—you remember who she is, of course?"

Delia doesn't nod.

"Chase's daughter. Your...granddaughter. She has no family now, no blood ties. I..." Another throat clear. "I won't live forever. And I just thought—I thought you should know that she's out there, on her own, and could probably use—"

"What do you want, money for her?"

"No. No! It's not that at all."

"Then what?"

"You have a big family, don't you? Chase had sisters? So there must be...there must be more of you. Cousins, grandchildren? People for her to call family."

"Do *you* want money, George?"

"For crying out— You are a horrible woman, you know that?" Oh, damn it, no, that's not what he meant to say. It's true, but now he's done it.

"I don't appreciate it when people come into my home and insult me to my face. General custom in the circles I travel in is to do it behind a person's back, but you wouldn't know that, would you, being of such low breeding? And I've heard you perfectly. But you're not making sense. What do you really want?"

George is feeling dizzy. He has to concentrate to breathe and then speak. "What I want is to know why, for all these years, you have refused to know her, when she's a blood relation of yours, when she's your *grandchild*. Is she not good enough for you, is that it? Because of Virginia, because of us? She's not even mine, you know. Virginia wasn't my daughter, she was the daughter of a close friend who died in the war, a hero, a brave man, a worthy man with better breeding than me."

At this, Delia's face registers surprise. She blinks a few times. George reaches into his wallet and takes out the photo he carries of Mae, taken at her college graduation. She's throwing her cap in the air and laughing into the camera. He extends his hand and tries to give the photo to Delia, but she doesn't take it, doesn't even look at it. "She's a wonderful girl. She's kind and honest and a good person, and she's your son's child. But she's lonely. She's a lonely person. And you're depriving her."

"Depriving her?" Her laugh is phlegmy, horrid. "She doesn't need me and she certainly doesn't need *us*. My son died a long time ago. And a lot died with him. Do you understand that? This is not the kind of family your Mae should want anything to do with. We are not warm. We are not welcoming. And we won't be, to her. Perhaps your grief is making you delusional. Our family despises yours, and we have our reasons."

He thinks of Lilly out there in the car and looks down at his shoes. "I'm not delusional."

She takes a step toward him. "You killed my son." He sways backward as if she's hit him. "You allowed those two to ride around in that boat, a boat that was put together by a drunk. What kind of an idiot allows his daughter to do that?"

He grabs his coat, then the dog's leash at his feet, makes it to the front door and out of the woman's house. He puts the dog in the back seat of the car and sits in the driver's seat, his heart pounding.

"It wasn't your fault, don't let her get to you," Lilly says to him. "She's just a mean, lonely old woman. There was nothing we could have done. Please, my love. Please believe that."

He does it, finally. He reaches out and tries to touch her cheek, but nothing is there. She's gone.

"Come back," he whispers.

But she won't. He knows it. This is it. He turns on the car and backs out of the driveway.

Do you have a whole crew of bored kids to entertain?

Have them put on a play.

Gabe leans up on one elbow and watches Mae in the moonlight that flows through the window when they sleep. She likes to leave the curtains open at night. Now the moonlight is annoying. It's keeping him awake.

He puts his head back down on the pillow and looks at the ceiling with its swirls of plaster from another era. He was dreaming, just now, of the baby. It was a boy, and Mae was holding him, and when Gabe looked closely, he realized it was him. And then he was in the cabin, and the baby wasn't a baby anymore. The baby was Gabe.

When he was five, Gabe found a photograph of his mother in a drawer.

"Is this her?" he asked Jonah. The woman had long hair and dark sad eyes. She was holding an infant.

"Yeah, it's her."

"Is that me?"

"That's you."

"Do you know where she went?"

"No damn clue. Don't give a shit either."

Gabe took the photograph into his room, slept with it on his pillow.

And then: "Wake up, you little asshole. Wake up."

Jonah stank of booze. He snatched the photo off Gabe's chest. "Give that back!" Gabe shouted.

"She wanted to take you, you dumb kid. Know that? She wanted you to go with her, and you said no. Don't you remember?"

"You're lying," Gabe said, then braced himself for the punch. But it didn't come. Not that time.

"You told her you couldn't leave me. You stupid, stupid little shit." Jonah ripped the picture in two, then three, then four. "I used to be like you, and then my dad got to me. You used to be better, and then I got to you. I wish you were never born."

"I'm never going to be like you," Gabe said, but he didn't believe it even then.

Jonah lifted the bottle he was holding. He said something unintelligible and stumbled out of the room. After a moment, Gabe could hear him outside, and after a while, there was the smash of his empty bottle against the cabin. The ground glittered out there, from all the broken glass right under Gabe's bedroom window. Gabe tried to see the photograph in his mind. One day, he'd find her. Maybe she'd gone to New York City. He wished hard that night that he'd get the chance one day to tell her he was sorry he didn't go with her.

Gabe stands, gets out of bed, dresses quietly and sneaks out the door. He's in the driveway of the inn now, his feet walking, but his mind numb.

He starts down the driveway. Did his mother walk away, just like this? After he left the bay for good, he used to eat at all the diners and dives he could find in New York City, because he had long imagined his mother as a waitress in the city, imagined that she had run away to a slightly better life, at least. He would know her because of the sad eyes he still remembered from the photograph. Except he never saw anyone he thought was her, not even for a second.

He checks his watch. It's past two a.m.; too late for a drink—but he wants one. He has wanted one, desperately, for days now. He walks faster. *Go away and don't come back.* It's Lilly's voice he hears now in his head. The things he will never be able to do for any child, and least of all a child who doesn't even belong to him. *Not enough. I'm not enough.* No matter what promise he made to Mae. Made to George. Made to himself.

He's nowhere near enough for this. He's not up to this. When Mae talks about the baby, when she describes hearing the heartbeat, when she starts discussing her plans for the nursery, he feels jealousy and resentment. He feels something black and rotten growing inside.

He stands on the riverbank and looks out at his father's island, but sees nothing but the night. He could put the island in her name, maybe. Then when it sold she could use the money to help take care of herself and the child. At least he could do that for her. That might help with the guilt. It might help him forget.

What a joke. He's never going to forget.

He turns and looks toward the inn; the porch light is shining. It would be so easy to go back there and get into bed with her and pretend he never left, that he never had these thoughts. They'll chase him, though. They're not going anywhere. Who he wants to be and who he really is are two different things. That ugliness, that part of himself he inherited from Jonah, is waiting just below the surface.

Things like this, they don't stay buried. "You taught me that, old man," Gabe says, turning back toward the river, and Island 51. "Thanks for nothing. I'll do what you want. But don't you fucking haunt them. You leave Mae and her baby alone, because I am."

There are canvases and art supplies on the screened-in
porch, in the basket in the corner.
While away the rainy day by painting something. It
doesn't matter if you don't know how—just try!

I'm sorry, Gabe's note reads. He's left it on his side of the bed. *I know this will be hard for you to understand, but you and the baby will be better off without me. I love you and I always will. I wish I'd said yes when you said we should just be friends. I can't believe I'm losing you again. I'm so sorry.*

She tears the note in half. Both halves say *I'm sorry.* She lets them fall to the floor.

Is it because she wouldn't let him see the baby? Is that what it is? She was lying there in the dark waiting for the technician to tell her the gestational age of the baby, and hoping so hard that some miracle would occur, that the technician would say, *You're barely four weeks pregnant, how did you even know?* And then she had wished they would call Gabe in, and she would tell him the good news, and everything would be right again.

When that didn't happen, she had started to cry. She couldn't speak, couldn't explain what was wrong to a stranger who stood in the dark, looking away politely because he'd probably experienced scenes like this before. When he finally asked if she wanted her partner to come in, she'd shaken her head no. And that had been that.

She forces herself out of bed. Downstairs in the kitchen she takes her morning-sickness pill, drinks juice, tea, eats half a

piece of toast, some sliced apple. She washes her single plate
and cup and puts them in the drying rack. She was so certain when she told Gabe she was going to keep this baby that
it was what she wanted. She kept thinking she'd be able to
make it work because she had to, because she had no family
and because this baby, no matter the imperfection of the situation, *was* her family. She had thought maybe Gabe would
be her family, too—and she had believed it, she really had.
She had believed in her and Gabe. She should have seen this
coming, but she didn't. Now he's gone, George is gone, Lilly
has been gone for some time. She's completely alone, and no
matter how many times she tells herself that's not really true,
that she has a companion, the baby inside her feels only like
an abstract idea, a distant flickering lighthouse she may never
reach—and when she does, what will become of her?

She walks to the fridge, looks at the calendar affixed there
with a magnet. It's Wednesday. There's a note on the square
date box that says she's supposed to go play bridge at Jean
Templeton's, whom she ran into at the flea market weeks
before, in another life. She and Gabe had been buying new
board games to replace all the ones in the games closet that
had missing pieces. Clue. Risk. Monopoly. An afternoon
stretched before them with nothing to do but play games and
be in love. "Ha." Mae's voice in the empty room startles her.
It sounds like someone else. Jean had hugged her and told her
how much they all missed Lilly, especially on Wednesdays,
especially at bridge, and Mae found herself telling Jean that
Lilly had taught her to play bridge years ago and that she'd
love to be their fourth, if they'd have her.

Bridge. Jean. Brownies. Make Jell-O salad. This is her
life now, these are her friends. Women in their eighties and
nineties who will die and break her heart, too, as soon as she
gets close to them.

"What's the point?" she asks the empty room. There's no answer, just the dripping of the faucet and the ticking of the clock. Gabe wrote that the baby would be better off without him, but he or she will probably be better off without Mae, too. "What kind of a mother can I be? What do I have to give?"

She walks to the window and looks out at the river. Rain is starting to fall on it in big fat drops. Endless rain, she's lost track of how many days it's been, and the river has been flowing faster, swelling bigger, every day. In some places, it rushes like rapids. It's unrecognizable, a new threat. There are warning signs all over town and along the riverbanks advising people to stay away from the water. Caution. Warning. Danger.

But Mae doesn't want to heed warnings anymore.

Her mother didn't.

Her grandmother didn't.

She walks to the lobby. She doesn't bother with a coat. She leaves the door wide open behind her because there's no one left to close it for.

Build a house of cards, then watch it collapse and try to build it up again.

George stops at a liquor store, then drives west until he's close to the airport, where there are rows of generic hotels. He checks in to the Holiday Inn. Do they put Gideon Bibles in hotel rooms anymore? Would it help him if they did? He slides open the drawer beside the bed. There's only a channel guide for the television there. *"The Lord is my shepherd; I shall not want."* It's the only Bible verse he can remember. And he's not the type of person to be comforted by words like that. He tried it on the ship the night it went down. He tried praying, too. And in the end, all he could do was close his eyes tight and whisper, "Lilly, Lilly, Lilly, Lilly." The only prayer he could believe in, the only thing that could lead him home.

He pours kibble into the ice bucket and watches the news while Bud eats. He fills the bathtub with water for Bud. He clicks the television off. He takes out the bottle of whiskey he bought, as well as the bottle of Percocet from when Lilly fell on a patch of ice and broke her wrist while out walking with Viv a few years ago. They've expired, but they'll do. He puts these two items on the bedside table and contemplates them. Then he pours some whiskey into a mug and dumps some pills into his hand. But he chokes on the pills when he tries to swallow them. He spits them into his hand, and they leave a chalky film on his palm. He dumps them into the toilet.

Too much of a coward, even to die. But there's always tomorrow.

Except tomorrow turns into three days in the hotel. Every night he takes one or two pills with a cup of whiskey. He doesn't eat. This will kill him eventually, won't it?

The room reeks of dog shit and urine. There is reproach in the dog's eyes when he looks at George, head hanging low. There are probably laws against this. "At least I'm feeding you," George snapped the night before. "Don't look at me like that." He's not proud that he's alienating the only friend he has left.

On the fourth morning, George wakes to the sound of pounding and barking.

"Go away!"

The knocking on the door continues. George thinks if he ignores it, whoever it is will go away, but to his shock the door swings open. He throws off the sheet and jumps up, stands there in his undershorts, mortified, caught. Dog shit, urine. The smell of his own unwashed body.

It's Delia. There's a security guard behind her. "Leave us," she commands, and the guard backs away. She strides into the room. "Disgusting," she says. "You're going to have to pay for this, you know."

Bud seems intimidated by her and cowers by the bed.

"Oh, for God's sake, put some clothes on." George is in his underwear. He doesn't know what else to do but pick up the dirty clothes he draped over the chair the night before and scuttle off to the bathroom to dress.

When he returns, she's standing beside the bed holding the whiskey and the pills.

"How did you find me?" he asks.

"I called your house, looking for you. A girl answered—

her, I assume. Said she didn't know where you were, that she hadn't heard from you in days. That doesn't seem to me like any way to treat your granddaughter."

"Get out," he manages.

She shakes the pill bottle. "How many of these did you take?"

"Maybe two…but over a period of time…"

"Ha!" She spits the laugh out at him. "Two Percocet and a sip of whiskey, and you thought *that* was going to kill you? That's just a regular night."

"It's a regular night for me, too," he mumbles.

"I suppose you had hoped that if you succeeded, I'd feel guilty," she says.

"I didn't think about you at all."

"And that's supposed to hurt me."

"Truly, you were the last thing on my mind." This is a lie. The truth: every night as he fell asleep, he heard her words in his head. *You killed my son.* If the pills and whiskey didn't kill him, he was sure those words were going to.

She prowls the room. "You can have anything if you have enough money, you know," she says. "That's why they let me up here when I had called enough hotels, when I finally found you. Anyone can be bought. When Anthony died I ended up with a lot of money, more money than I will ever know what to do with. And I can have anything, but there's nothing I really want." She looks thoughtful. "You hate this place, don't you?" He nods and sits down on the bed. The dog curls protectively around his bare feet. "Yet you won't go home."

"There is nothing to go back to. Mae—she hates me. And Lilly, gone, never loved me."

"That's a stupid thing to say. Of course she loved you."

"You don't know anything about this and I'm not interested in your commentary."

She adjusts the fur coat draped over her shoulders like a cape. "I came back to Alexandria Bay once, you know. Maybe fifteen years ago, over Christmas. I remember driving through that same old archway, the one that says 'Heart of the Thousand Islands,' and realizing the place hadn't changed. That hurt. It brought it all back. I drove to your inn, and I sat outside and idled the car for a while. Then I drove back through town to that bland Holiday Inn on the outskirts."

George frowns at her.

"Later, I worked up the stomach to drive back into town. I parked a bit down the road from the inn. I saw your girl outside, shoveling the snow. I knew it was her. I watched her for a while."

George feels tired. He lies back and stares up at the ceiling. He feels like a child being told a bedtime story. And it's better not having to look at her. Her voice, when it is separate from her cruel, ruined face, is almost pleasant. Husky, sad, wise, like an aging starlet.

"After a while, I saw her go inside, and then she came out and walked down the road, straight past my car and over to the community center. So I waited, and then I got out of the car and I went there, too. The door was locked. I peered inside and spotted her, passing by with a bunch of papers in her hands and then stopping, startled, when she saw my face. She opened the door for me. I searched her face for signs, for any resemblance to my son. She looks just like Virginia, doesn't she? But absolutely nothing like Chase. I said to her, I'm just visiting and I was wondering what's going on here at the community center."

A weight on the bed beside George. Bud has joined him.

He reaches out his hand, places it on the customary spot, just below his neck.

"She told me there was a matinee, a community theater production of *Romeo and Juliet*, for Christmas. She said she was the props manager and the stage manager because she was going to go to business school in the spring. I felt proud in that moment, George. A girl with a head on her shoulders."

"She has a name," he says, his eyes closed.

Delia ignores him. "I went to the play. You were there, but you didn't recognize me. You sat there with Lilly, held your wife's hand and acted like every single thing your grand-daughter did or said was the absolute most brilliant thing any-one had ever done or said."

He remembers how Mae had pulled it all together so well and given a little speech at the end. He can picture it. And, yes, he was proud of her.

"Is this is why you came here? To tell me that you enjoyed the community theater production you saw in my town?"

"At the end, the scene where Lady Montague says that the death of her son has shriveled her, or something like that—that it was like a bell, beginning to toll her doom. I almost left the room then, but I didn't want to draw attention to myself. But that was it, that was the moment I realized I was never going to feel better, ever. The death of my son shriv-eled me up. I died when he did, but I was forced to keep on living. And there it is, George. The end. *Finis*."

He lies there, stays motionless, his hand on the dog's neck. It wasn't the story he had hoped for. "I prefer a happy end-ing," he says.

She's still holding the whiskey and the pills. "I don't have a happy ending for me. Maybe for you, though."

"Not possible."

"You really don't understand, do you? Families have secrets. But most have no power at all." She shakes the bottle at him. "Don't be a coward. You may not feel it right now, but you do have something to live for. You're lucky. And, George?" She says it in a way that startles him. He sits up on the bed and there's her face again, but her voice is different now.

"If I'd been a better mother, maybe I would have raised a boy who didn't drink too much, who didn't shrink from his responsibilities. But I wasn't. And my remaining children, I didn't do such a good job with them either. You don't want Mae coming into this fold. Trust me. Please."

Her voice—a despair he recognizes.

"No one could have done anything differently," he says.

"Do you really believe that?"

He thinks of Lilly in the car. "Yes," he says.

"Then stop blaming yourself. Let me have my unhappy ending. Let me protect Mae from the vicious cycle our family became. I care about what happens to her, but it will always be from afar. You go back to her. Her family, it's you."

There are some nice new coffeehouses in town.
Go and drink so much coffee your hands start to shake.

Gabe is sitting at his laptop positioned at a small desk in front of his new apartment's only window—which is at least a large one—watching two men on the street below argue over a parking space. One of them has a kid in his car with him and he's swearing so loudly Gabe can hear him through the window.

He can't focus. He's been home for almost two weeks, and finally last night he went out with a few of his buddies, finally announced to everyone that he was back. He didn't drink—he's not going to, ever again—but he stayed out late. His friends offered their condolences about his father when he used that as an explanation for why he'd been out of town for so long, and they all sat in silent reflection for a moment. Gabe had never told any of them about his relationship with Jonah, aside from the fact that they didn't talk much. This was a relief, not having to get into it. A few minutes passed, and then they moved on to discussing the Knicks.

Maybe therapy would help. He did try it, once. Natasha insisted on it. "You're like a...like a cake," the therapist had said. "A cake that had the oven opened on it at a critical moment, when it was just starting to rise. So, you know, it slumped." He'd never gone back after that. No more therapy, ever. He'll go for a walk instead.

He ends up in front of the American Museum of Natural History, a place he used to visit often when he first arrived in New York City years ago. Of all the aphorisms on the walls, Gabe at eighteen was most struck by the words about manhood: "It is hard to fail, but it is worse never to have tried to succeed. All daring and courage, all iron endurance of misfortune make for a finer, nobler type of manhood."

Now his eyes land on the last words: "Only those are fit to live who do not fear to die and none are fit to die who have shrunk from the joy of life and the duty of life." *The duty of life.* He shoves his hands deep in his pockets. He did do his duty, by leaving Alexandria Bay. So why does he feel like such a shit?

He turns away from the rotunda and looks at an allosaurus skeleton towering over its baby, defending it against a predator. It's naïveté that prompted the paleontologists to display the bones in this fashion. It's not always like this, he knows. His own mother probably died on the streets, an addict, a prostitute. That down-on-her-luck diner waitress with the heart of gold—she never existed.

He closes his eyes against this, but every time he closes them, Mae's face is there.

She's going to be a great mother. A perfect one. She'll never let the heartache of life, the pain of existing, take away her hope. She'll be the type to do anything for her child, no matter how hard things get. And things will get easier for her. It's just a matter of time. She's not going to be alone for long. She'll find someone. Someone better. Mae is the type of woman people fall in love with.

God, how he misses her. He wants to hide from the world, wants never to have to see another face that isn't hers.

He walks back through the pillars and out onto the street. His phone starts to ring. It's the phone number of the inn. His heart flies high above the city skyscrapers. He fumbles with the phone and says, "Hello?" in a voice he didn't know could still be his.

It's not her, though. It's George. And he sounds upset. "Gabe, you need to come back."

If you can't round up some other guests for a round of bridge, euchre or crazy eights, play solitaire.

What drew Mae away from the river? She was so close she could feel the freedom of it, no despair, no fear; she was so close she could almost taste the release—and then it wasn't raining anymore. The sun edged its way out from behind a cloud that had, moments before, seemed so dense there was the possibility the sun would never be seen again, at least not by Mae, whose intentions had been so clear. Until everything had changed. She had gasped and stumbled backward, and the water that would have taken hold of her had rushed past without her.

It was her parents' island, she supposes—when she allows herself to think of the moment at all, which is less and less with each day that passes—that brought her back. She saw not its shape but the idea of it, the tips of the pine trees she knew skirted the little bay beyond which the ruined foundation of the fishing camp sat. She knew she wasn't alone, understood suddenly that it didn't matter if she couldn't remember very much about her mother. Her mother had loved her. She had loved her so much. And part of the reason she had loved her so much was because Mae, simply by existing, had made it so that Virginia had never been alone, even in her most difficult moments.

Mae had placed her hand on her stomach. *I'm sorry.* And she had known that, just as she forgave her parents for their mistakes, just as Gabe, in his way, had forgiven his father for his mistakes over and over, had crossed the river so many times in the hopes that things would be different, her child would forgive her for this.

What was important now was for Mae to make sure there weren't too many things to forgive.

She had stretched her hand out toward the islands she could now see in the clearing mist. "There," she had said to the child in her future. "There are the islands." She pointed at Island 51 and her hand shook but she kept it held high. "Gabe lived there. He was my best friend. And I miss him." She would tell the story of Gabe to the baby one day. She would talk about her friend, the lost boy. She would not let the hurt of it color the memory. Because if she didn't talk about Gabe, she wouldn't be able to talk about her own childhood. She wouldn't be able to tie a new rope to the old oak tree on the shore and say to her child that once, a long time ago, she swung on this rope with a friend and she was happy.

It was her parents' island that had brought her back, but it was also herself. She was the one who stepped away from the water. There was no one there to save her, and so she saved herself. She turned away from the river, walked down the road, splashed through the puddles, and went home. She knew, finally, why her mother had loved the rain so much. It wasn't perfect; it didn't have to be. When it rained, everything else was washed away. Everything you did that day became a gift, sometimes even an act of bravery that no one else would know about, ever, because everyone else was hiding inside.

It wasn't easy. Even if she wasn't really alone, even if the child was there with her, silently waiting, even if she had Viv, and the bridge ladies, it wasn't easy to keep her loneliness at bay. At night, in her bed without Gabe, that was the worst time. She tried sleeping in other rooms but he was in all of them. She gave up and decided to wait. Time would heal this, wouldn't it?

She went for a walk every day in the opposite direction from the path she had followed that dark afternoon. And every day, as she returned home to the empty inn, she felt a little better. But she also felt surprised, with every passing day, that Gabe hadn't returned.

Then, late one afternoon, as she rounded the corner on the road that led her to the inn's driveway, she heard a barking dog. Not Gabe, no. But hope.

George's Buick is there, and Bud is running around the yard. He's covered in mud, he's digging holes happily, he's peeing against the birdbath once again. Mae starts to run, through the mud, through the rain that has started up again, but more softly. She runs through the imperfect world she lives in, the one her child will soon live in. It's the only world she has to offer. She'll have to try to find a way to explain that one day, without making happiness seem impossible.

"I'm sorry," George begins. He's about to say, "And there are things you need to know," but she interrupts him, points down at her stomach.

"You're going to be a great-grandfather."

There are some interesting monuments around town.

Grab an umbrella and go check them out.

"We should go to the cemetery," George says to Mae. "Will we walk, or drive? How do you feel?" A child. It's given him one more thing to fear. Will he lose both her and this child once he tells her the truth?

"Let's walk, I need the exercise," she says. "Now that the morning sickness has stopped all I do is eat."

When he stops in front of Everett's grave, she's confused, but before she can ask, he begins to explain, speaks quickly so he won't lose his courage. "You're not my blood, Mae. I'm so sorry." He's crying and ashamed. The words do not flow. He sounds halting, and old. But there had been fear in Mae's eyes when he began his story—and he sees that it's gone now.

"I thought it was something horrible," she says. "I thought maybe you were going to tell me you were sick, that you were... It doesn't matter. This changes nothing about the way I feel about you. You can't think this changes anything."

"It doesn't?"

"Of course not. There's more than one way to be a family with someone." In the silence, George knows she's thinking of Gabe. She told him he was gone, after she told him about the baby. He hadn't known what to say, and he still doesn't. He reaches for her hand. When she forces a smile, she reminds him of Lilly and Virginia. Durable strength, like precious metal. Precious, this person. His girl, no matter what.

"Everett was your brother. He wasn't blood, but he was still your brother. I understand that. I do."

But there's more. He doesn't deserve forgiveness yet. He has to tell her about Lilly. He lets go of her hand and points down at the ground before them. "We don't have your grandmother's ashes anymore. They're gone. I dumped them here, out of spite, I guess. I'm sorry. I've hidden things from you and taken liberties that weren't mine to take."

"That doesn't matter. Her ashes, they weren't her. I feel her here. Is that crazy?"

He thinks about Lilly, with him in the car.

"No, that's not crazy" is all he says.

Back at the inn, he unpacks the car, carries his small suitcase inside, a bag of food for the poor dog who has remained unchanged in his loyalty to George no matter what he's put him through, and Lilly's cedar box. He presents it to Mae. "This was hers. There are things in here that are difficult to talk about, but if you want to talk about them, I will."

"Oh," Mae breathes. "Are some of my mother's things in here? You can't imagine what a gift this is."

That night, they build a fire. Mae sifts through the box, and he watches the news with the dog at his feet. There's not peace in the world, there never seems to be, but there's peace here, in this room. There's Mae, there's the fire, there's the time that has passed, there's what's still to come. He'll have to be brave because growing old isn't for the faint of heart. Lilly always used to say that. He finds himself smiling. "You got out while you still could," he whispers, because he hasn't gotten used to not talking to her.

One final thing, though. He remembers one last thing he

took that wasn't his, and he's happy to have it. Once Mae goes to bed he reaches into his breast pocket, draws out the paper he keeps there. Someone needs to set Gabe straight. Someone needs to be a father to him, to lay down the law, to bring him into their family once and for all.

Once George has finished speaking with Gabe, once he's satisfied that he has been heard and will be obeyed—and once he has been reassured, also, that this boy loves Mae as much as George has always believed he did—he hangs up and goes to stand by the window in the kitchen. The moon is shining on the river. Mae said it was quite the rain they had, that the river was wild for a while, but there's hardly any trace of that now save some debris still dotted along the shore. Everything will go back to the way it was. Spring is here, and he's lived to see another one. He'll likely live to see another summer, too, and the birth of his great-grandson or -granddaughter in the fall. What a brave girl that Mae is. Just like her mother. Just like Lilly.

"It's been a very good day," he says to Lilly. He waits for a moment, can't help but be hopeful because he's alone now, but she doesn't materialize. That's all right. He'll see Lilly again someday. And meanwhile, he's had a good day. That's quite a thing for a person who was certain he had none of those left.

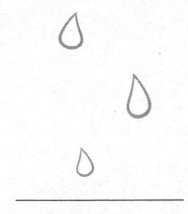

Eventually, the rain is going to stop.

It always does.

Just wait, if that's all you feel like doing.

Just watch, and wait.

In the afternoon, as Mae passes the front window, she sees Gabe on the driveway and she's not surprised. It didn't get easier. She didn't stop believing he was going to come back. And here he is. She didn't need him to return, she knew she would have survived without him—but she also knew him well enough to hope he would return and not allow that hope to stop. She stands and watches him until he disappears up the stairs, until he knocks.

She opens the door. She says, first, "I've been taking your boat out. I'm not afraid anymore. I learned to drive it."

"That's great. Mae, I—"

"Don't say you're sorry and don't make me any promises. Let's just take things one day at a time."

They don't touch each other, not right away. They face each other, waiting to not be afraid. That moment never comes, so they reach beyond it.

"Forever," he says, holding her close. "One day at a time, forever."

EPILOGUE

LIFE GOES ON.

Tonight, when Mae was watching the news, a report came on about a volcano that had suddenly erupted in Japan while there were hikers on the mountain. People perished. Mae has to turn the sound up so loud to hear it now that Gabe had to put a door on the den, but he says he doesn't mind, he likes to do things around the place to feel relevant.

Her boys laugh at her loud nights in front of the television when they come to visit, because apparently almost no one watches television anymore—but they do come to visit, a lot. And her boys have children, boys of their own, and now those boys have their own little boys. So many boys. How does that happen in families? You don't always get what you think you want, but sometimes you get more than you ever could have imagined.

"GG!" (That's what they call her, short for "Great-grandma.") "The volume's too loud!" the little boys will shout when she's watching TV. They're very loud themselves, so that's something, to be called loud by these boys.

Mae will cup her ear and shout, "What's that? I can't hear you. Come closer!" When they do, she grabs one or the other and tickles them until they roll on the floor in fits of laughter. She'll look at their tiny bodies, hear them laughing and watch them rolling on the floor, and she'll think, *Well, there you have it. Life goes on. And on and on.* This is something you learn when you're as old as she is now.

A friend dies, but for Mae and Gabe, life goes on. Another friend dies, and it's the same. Other things in the bay go on, deaths and births and changes—but mostly deaths these days. She's past 90 years old now and can imagine her end, but she doesn't fear it. Bravery is in the living. Her grandfather George told her this before he died—at 102.

She doesn't know if she'll live that long but it would seem there's longevity in the family if she's gone on this far. It doesn't matter, though. She doesn't count the days. She just tries to feel grateful for every one, for every moment, for all the small things. Every time she sees a shooting star, for example, she'll say, "Well, another one didn't hit us," and Gabe, he'll laugh, that familiar chuckle she loves so much. And he'll give her a kiss, and they'll remember their first one.

It's been a good life. It has. Sure, there have been troubles, mostly at the beginning, and some around the middle, too. One day at a time, forever. Forever has come and gone, and they're still here, she and Gabe, making the same promise day after day, without any words.

Has her relationship with Gabe always been perfect? No. Like her life, it hasn't. Has she always done the right thing? Most of the time, but definitely not always. For example, she never told Lawrence, her firstborn son, who his father really was. She kept thinking she would, but, like her grandmother before her, she ended up getting lost in the thing that felt the most true. Gabe acted as Lawrence's father—they had named him together, after the river; his eyes were the same color, they agreed, as the river in spring—and there never seemed

to be a right moment to tell him his biological father was a
man in prison. Then George Jr. was born. After that, Mae
feared the revelation might tear the two of them apart when
they were so close—so what would be the point? The secret
grew large for a while, in Mae's mind. It kept her up at night,
the idea that there were people in the world who would judge
her choice if they knew what she was concealing.

But no one did know. Only Gabe. It kept them close. Con-
spirators. Every marriage harbors secrets, secrets about why
it works or why it doesn't work, secrets between two people
that the rest of the world can never be privy to. These are
theirs: that blood isn't everything; that families can be cho-
sen; that love doesn't come naturally, that it's not supposed
to; that choosing love is sometimes better than giving it out
of obligation.

She's kept tabs on Peter over the years, mostly to make sure
there weren't any health concerns she needed to know about,
nothing that could have been passed along to Lawrence. As
far as she knows, he's still alive, out of jail and living a no-
account existence back in Novi. Had he ever dared to come
and find her in the bay, he never would have found a single
clue by looking into Lawrence's river-green eyes. "Everyone has done at least one thing they're not proud of that they
need to forgive themselves for," she might have said, had he
come around. She might even have said she forgave him for
what he'd done, might have told him it didn't matter anymore, might have suggested he try to forgive himself. This
simple truth about forgiveness, she keeps it to herself. And
she shares it with Gabe, whenever it seems he might need to
be reminded.

Tonight, she and Gabe are going out for their customary
walk along the river. It starts to snow, but Mae doesn't pull the
hood of her parka up over her white hair. Her mother loved

the rain, but she has grown to love the snow. "Shall we go check on the river?" she asks her husband. They make their way toward the stairs and carefully descend. They look out at the dark islands. Her parents' island was sold, and so was Island 51. That money kept them afloat over the years, kept the inn running and shaped their lives. There are families on those islands now who make memories every summer. Mae doesn't know who they are, but she's sure they have stories of their own, happy, sad, somewhere in between. And they have those islands, to keep their stories safe. Sometimes she feels jealous of this, feels those islands should contain only her stories, and Gabe's stories. But islands don't really belong to anyone. Letting them go was the right thing to do.

"Time to go?" Gabe asks, and she tears her gaze away from the invisible past.

"Thank you," she says as he helps her back up the stairs. She doesn't know what she'll do without him if he dies first. She tries not to think about this. Everything ends, eventually. You can't be afraid of that, because that's just life, and you have to live it, find the beauty in it, stop worrying all the time about silly things like whether it might rain and focus on what's important, like whether the people you love know how much you love them, whether you can still picture the people you've lost when you close your eyes at night, and whether you remembered to check on the river when you walked past it that day, to make sure it was still flowing in the right direction, carrying your past, present and future together in one miraculous moment that will go on, always, with you or without you.

★ ★ ★ ★ ★

ACKNOWLEDGMENTS

I AM GRATEFUL TO THE FOLLOWING PEOPLE:

My agent Samantha Haywood, an excellent person, all around (I'd say I'm your biggest fan but I think my dad has dibs on that); Stephanie Sinclair, a generous, openhearted first reader; and the rest of the team at Transatlantic Agency, for taking care of details big and small. Plus Hannah Fosh, who lit up my life.

At Simon & Schuster Canada, Nita Pronovost, who saw this book for what it could be and helped me find the right stepping stones; Sarah St. Pierre, for many kindnesses; Siobhan Doody, for getting this book to the finish line; Amy Prentice, a true professional (I miss you!); Adria Iwasutiak, for encouragement and heart-to-hearts; Felicia Quon, for baskets of beaches and buckets of laughs; David Millar, for always making me feel welcome; Kevin Hanson, for steering the ship with a sure hand; Sherry Lee and Shara Alexa, for tirelessly ensuring my books end up on shelves; Elizabeth Whitehead, for the charming cover; and the rest of the S&S family: Jacquelynne Lennard, Loretta Eldridge, Andrea Seto, Alexandra Boelsterli, Brendan May.

At Graydon House, Brittany Lavery, for giving me the benefit of your keen editorial eye—and for your constant willingness to discuss baseball and/or cats; Dianne Moggy and Susan Swinwood, for a warm welcome; Michelle Renaud and Amy Jones, for passion and unstinting vision; Kathleen Oudit and the artist Kazuko Nomoto for the original cover concept—and Kathleen, Erin Craig and Karen Becker for making the final (beautiful) version work. At Rowohlt, I am grateful to Silke Jellinghaus and her enthusiastic colleagues Katharina Dornhoefer, Suenje Redies and Ulrike Beck; and to Katharina Naumann.

My coven of lady writers, who are always in my corner (lucky me!) and I am deeply proud to call my friends: Karma Brown, Chantel Guertin, Kate Hilton, Jennifer Robson, Elizabeth Renzetti. Thank you also to my dear friend Sherri Vanderveen for hearing my voice in my writing and liking it; and to Leigh Andre, Amanda Watson and Michelle Schlag.

Early readers Danila Botha (heart emoji), Sophie Chouinard, Alison Clarke, Moriah Cleveland, Amanpreet Dhami, Asha Frost (you're magical), Ellen Nodwell and Nance Williams. Forgive me if I've forgotten anyone. This book has had some past lives.

Booksellers everywhere, and especially Sarah Ramsey, Kathy Chant and Shelley Macbeth. Long may you run.

My readers. You. Because without you there would be no this. Believe me when I say there is a moment in every day within which I pause and marvel over how fortunate I am to get to share my writing with an audience that doesn't consist solely of my parents and my husband. So if you're holding this book and you're not my parents or my husband, thank you. I'm honoured.

My grandparents, in loving memory: Ray, for singing "That Sly Old Gentleman" and giving us a song to pass down generation by generation (to be used at the end of each day, when it counts the most); Maggie, because if a writing gene exists you passed yours to me (oh, how I wish you could read these books); Ron, for always watching out for me, and for being so proud of us all; Jean, for the unconditional love and the stiff upper lip (I miss you every single day; the kids still remember the baths); and Lawrence: I wish I had met you. You are never forgotten. Now I've made sure.

The Soper family—especially my uncles for starting that book club. I look forward to the next meeting. Extra thanks to Gary for the photos.

The Stapley family, and especially my supportive tribe of aunts and uncles. Special thanks to Auntie Di who hosted me in Gananoque as I researched the St. Lawrence River and its islands and sought solitude to write. You understood what I needed and you gave it to me.

Randy Greenman, for the photographs and clippings, and his assistance in keeping Lawrence's legacy alive.

My parents: Bruce Stapley, for endless support, for long talks, for the necklace and the silly song. My mom, Valerie Clubine, who first showed me what a mother's love meant so I could write about it the way I have; James Clubine, my stepfather, for your reassurance and love. I'd be lost (literally, wandering around in the night; ask Mom) without all of you. And to my brothers, Shane, Drew and Griffin. I do sometimes wish you'd been sisters instead, but I love you an awful lot just the same.

My Ponikowski parents: Joyce and Joe Sr., for being as proud of me as you would be of your own daughter; and to the rest of the Ponikowski and Webb families.

Oscar, for the good luck and the healing snuggles.

Joseph and Maia. If you ever read this book and you get to the parts about how much Virginia loved Mae and how much Lilly loved Virginia then you might be at the very beginning of understanding how much I love the two of you. You always make me feel I'm doing something right because truly, you are the most wonderful people. I promise to always have candy at my book launches. I promise never to stop sneaking into your rooms to watch you sleep. I promise to tell you stories about yourselves until I can't remember them anymore. I promise to love you exactly as you are and for exactly who you are, always.

And, Joe. Love is a choice. We've learned that, haven't we? And I choose you, I always have. Thank you for choosing me back, and for everything else. Yet again, this could not have been completed without you. Nor could the laundry. I'm grateful for that, too.

ABOUT THE AUTHOR

Marissa Stapley, bestselling author of *Mating for Life*, is a newspaper journalist and a National Magazine Award–nominated magazine writer. Her book reviews appear regularly in the *Toronto Star*, and she writes a commercial fiction review column, Shelf Love, for the *Globe and Mail*. She has also taught creative writing at the University of Toronto and editing at Centennial College. She lives in Toronto with her husband and two children. Visit her at www.marissastapley.com or follow her on Twitter @marissastapley.

QUESTIONS FOR DISCUSSION

1. What does *family* mean to you? Is family something you're born into or something you can create?

2. Describe the relationship Mae and her fiancé, Peter, had. Do you believe he ever loved her? What does Mae learn from their interactions?

3. The St. Lawrence River is a character in and of itself in this novel. How would you describe its role in the story and its effect on the various characters?

4. Do you think it's possible for teenage sweethearts to pick up where they left off? How do time and maturity change our outlook on life and our relationships with others?

5. What role do love and jealousy play in the novel?

6. Gabe comes from a family that has a legacy of alcoholism and abuse. How does he view himself in light of that? Do you think that makes him a different person than he might

otherwise have been? How does his past affect the decisions he makes?

7. Lilly hurt George by accidentally revealing the truth about Virginia's paternity. What would you have done in George's situation? Was Lilly right to have hidden the truth from him all these years?

8. Lilly's actions have an enormous effect on her granddaughter's life. In your opinion, were those actions justified? Why do you think she tells Gabe "Mae is not for you"? How much regret do you believe she feels and in what ways does that regret change her?

9. Why does George befriend Jonah so late in both their lives? Do they have anything in common besides their shared family history? What influence, if any, do they have on each other?

10. Does Mae's character change as the story progresses? If so, how?

11. Do you agree with Gabe's decision not to tell George about Lilly's lie? Why or why not? What would you have done in the same situation?

12. In your opinion, why does Gabe hold himself responsible for the deaths of Mae's parents?

A CONVERSATION
WITH MARISSA STAPLEY

1. *Things to Do When It's Raining* is such a heartfelt portrayal of love in all its forms. What was your inspiration for writing this novel?

I was very close to my grandparents growing up, but my grandfather and I were not biologically related. My grandmother's first husband, Lawrence, died tragically when my mother was two, and it remains a painful topic for both families. As such, I knew that Lawrence had existed, and had seen movie-star-handsome pictures of him with my grandmother Jean—they looked so in love! The photos inspired many stories, but I had few concrete details about Lawrence.

After my grandmother passed away in 2013, a few things happened to get me thinking about writing this story. Lawrence's brother attended Jean's funeral, and I introduced him to one of my younger cousins as my great-uncle. She later told me she was shocked; she hadn't known about Lawrence. He had become a secret

> "They looked
> so in love!"

because his death was too painful to discuss. Better to bury it, we had all decided—without saying a word.

I also saw how lost and alone my grandfather was without Jean. Perhaps they hadn't had a Hollywood-worthy love story, but he was a childhood friend before they married, so their story had its own sweetness. He married Jean, a widow with a young child, and in doing so he had saved her, and she saved him, too. I had always imagined the love story as being between my grandmother and poor, lost Lawrence. But Jean's death made me realize that, despite the devastating loss of her first husband, she had carried on. Ultimately, she had developed a very deep bond with the man with whom she would spend the rest of her life. When she died, she was calling for *him*.

And so, I started writing. It helped to write a character like Lilly because I felt my grandmother was with me as I wrote. My grandfather died shortly after her, and this book has really turned into my way of saying goodbye to all of them and ensuring they live on in some way.

2. Why did you choose the Summers' Inn as the setting for the novel?

I always seem to go to water when I'm looking for inspiration. As I began the challenging task of starting a second novel, I spent some time in Gananoque, Ontario, visiting an aunt who lives near the river. I needed a setting that was a character in itself, a setting that would tie the characters together—characters painfully close to my heart because they were inspired by real people I had loved.

"I needed a setting that was a character in itself."

The inn took shape alongside the Summers family. I realized they needed a naturally hospitable home, open to someone like Gabe, especially. It made sense that he would live there, that Mae would gravitate there, and that Lilly and George would be so tied to it. I had even envisioned drawing some of the guests into the story, but once I got to know George, Lilly, Gabe and Mae, I realized I was going to have my hands full—these were complicated people.

3. Do you like the rain? What is your favorite thing to do when it's raining?

My mother always said that we couldn't let bad weather ruin our day. So although I wouldn't say I *love* the rain, I welcome it. There's something more satisfying about accomplishing things on a rainy day than on a regular day. Sunshine is easy; rain is a challenge.

I'm also the kind of person who forgets to pack an umbrella, so I'm always walking through rain with my face upturned, with that Roger Miller quote running through my head: "Some people feel the rain; others just get wet." I think Virginia's character was born on a rainy walk home from

> "But choosing to love, even when it's difficult, is often the most rewarding choice."

school, as I laughed my way through a rainstorm alongside my young daughter. Virginia so badly wanted her child to be resilient, to weather life's rainstorms, and to simply turn her face toward the raindrops and laugh at them.

My favorite thing to do when it's raining is to cuddle up with a book, preferably with my kids and kitten nearby, also reading—well, not the kitten. He doesn't know how to read yet.

4. In the book you write that "Choosing love is sometimes better than giving it out of obligation." Is this something you've learned from your own experience?

I think everyone learns that—with families, marriages, long friendships and with their children. New love and new relationships, those are easy! It's when you really get to know someone and when they hurt you a few times—because that's what people do by virtue of who we are—that you either decide to work on it or you quit it altogether. But choosing to love, even when it's difficult, is often the most rewarding choice. I think we really see that in this novel because everyone has to *choose* to love one another. There are points where walking away was probably the easier option, but that makes the ultimate decision to choose love a brave one.

5. The St. Lawrence River plays such a big part in Mae and Gabe's life. Did you grow up around water? Have you ever been afraid of water?

I didn't grow up around water, but we spent a lot of time around water on family vacations. I think I've always associated being around water with being truly relaxed and at peace.

Yes, I'm actually very nervous, not of water itself, but of what might be in the water. I'm terrified of muskie, and when I was a kid, my older brother loved to torture me with his knowledge of this fear. I'm terrified of seaweed, too. It's an incredibly irrational fear! Yet I persist; I will swim anywhere. As I get older, I spend more time just plunging in. My fears don't exactly go away, but they matter less.

6. Mae has such a close relationship with her grandparents Lilly and George. Were you close with your grandparents growing up?

Very! I was especially close with my mother's parents, but I did have a special connection to my father's mom, Grannie Maggie, who was a prolific Canadian magazine writer and would have been so thrilled to see my books published.

My maternal grandparents were like a second set of parents, just as Lilly and George are to Mae. I lived with them during university and would forgo meeting my friends at the pub after class so I could rush home in time for our daily routine of watching *Wheel of Fortune* and *Jeopardy!* together while eating dinner on our laps. They were the kind of people you would describe as "salt of the earth." Not a day goes by that I don't wish they were still here.

> "My grandparents were like a second set of parents."

7. Now that you've finished writing the book, is there a character you wish you could revisit, or is there a character with whom you most identify?

I miss them all: Lilly because she reminds me of my grandmother, George because he reminds me of my grandfather, and Mae because I definitely identify with her as a person. Then there's Gabe—I think about him all the time. It's probably time to admit I have a crush on someone who doesn't exist.

> "I know I can never revisit him because there will never be any more to know about him than what is already on paper—but that doesn't stop me from wishing it could be different."

If I had to choose one character from the book to revisit, it would be Everett. Just as my biological grandfather is essentially unknowable to me and my mother, Everett was always outside of my grasp as a character, too. He didn't live long enough for anyone to know him beyond the rather careless days of his youth. And yet, he touched the lives of each character in some way. I know I can never revisit him because there will never be any more to know about him than what is already on paper—but that doesn't stop me from wishing it could be different.

PHOTOS

My Grandpa Ron Soper, in a photo taken around 1947. He and my grandmother grew up in Dundalk, Ontario together and were childhood friends before they married in 1954

Lawrence Greenman, my biological grandfather, in 1944. He was a POW for a year in WWII (and in this photo had no idea what was in store for him), making his tragic death at twenty-eight years old in a workplace accident even more heartbreaking.

Grandma Jean and her new husband, Lawrence, departing for their honeymoon to Banff in 1948. In the background, Lawrence's father, my mother's "Grandpa George," can be seen.

My beloved grandmother Jean McIntyre, standing on the steps of a hospital in Collingwood, Ontario, where she was training to be a nurse. This was around the time she met Lawrence, at a New Year's Eve dance.